"I'm pregnant."

Despite being prepared to █████████ still stuttered when she actually ████ ████ █████ pregnant. They'd made a child together. Conflicting emotions battered him on every side.

"Say something." Joni's voice reeked of desperation, a sound he'd never wanted to hear from her.

"I don't know what to say."

He remembered every blissful second of their night together. It had been one of the best nights of his life. And it had cost him the most important relationship in his life. Though Lex had tried to put things back the way they'd been the morning after he and Joni had made love by apologizing and suggesting they pretend that nothing had happened, it hadn't worked. The easy comfort they'd shared was gone. He was trying to become her friend again, but she wasn't interested.

Now that she was pregnant there was no way they could pretend that night hadn't happened and go back to being best friends. Unfortunately he didn't know what kind of relationship they could have in the future.

The child would always be proof that for at least one night they'd been lovers.

* * *

SWEET BRIAR SWEETHEARTS:
There's something about Sweet Briar...

Dear Reader,

Have you ever met people who you knew belonged together? A couple so perfect that you could almost see the love connecting them? That's exactly how I felt about Joni Danielson and Lex Devlin, the heroine and hero of the latest book in my Sweet Briar Sweethearts series. I knew from the first time I saw them together in *How to Steal the Lawman's Heart* that they would be perfect together. They were good friends and fit together like puzzle pieces. Everything between them was so easy. So relaxed. When it came time to tell their story, I wanted them to look into each other's eyes and declare their love.

But where's the fun in that? Sure, I wanted Joni and Lex to live happily ever after, but first they and their relationship had to be tested. Although they knew each other quite well, there were things they didn't know about each other or themselves. Things they would never know if the path of their relationship was too smooth. So I gave them some trouble. The road was rocky for a while, but when they finally reached their happily-ever-after, they were able to know their love had been tested and they were stronger for it.

I love hearing from my readers. Please feel free to visit my website, kathydouglassbooks.com, and drop me a note. While you're there, sign up for my newsletter. That way I'll be able to keep in touch with you.

I'm also on Facebook at Author Kathy Douglass. Stop by and say hi. Or if you prefer Twitter, I'm there, too, @kathydouglass7.

Best wishes and happy reading!

Kathy

A Baby
Between Friends

———

Kathy Douglass

HARLEQUIN® SPECIAL EDITION

Recycling programs
for this product may
not exist in your area.

ISBN-13: 978-1-335-57405-3

A Baby Between Friends

Copyright © 2019 by Kathleen Gregory

This edition published by arrangement with Harlequin Books S.A.

For questions and comments about the quality of this book,
please contact us at CustomerService@Harlequin.com.

® and TM are trademarks of Harlequin Enterprises Limited or its
corporate affiliates. Trademarks indicated with ® are registered in the
United States Patent and Trademark Office, the Canadian Intellectual
Property Office and in other countries.

Printed in U.S.A.

Kathy Douglass came by her love of reading naturally—both of her parents were readers. She would finish one book and pick up another. Then she attended law school and traded romances for legal opinions.

After the birth of her two children, her love of reading turned into a love of writing. Kathy now spends her days writing the small-town contemporary novels she enjoys reading.

Books by Kathy Douglass

Harlequin Special Edition

Sweet Briar Sweethearts

How to Steal the Lawman's Heart
The Waitress's Secret
The Rancher and the City Girl
Winning Charlotte Back
The Rancher's Return
A Baby Between Friends

Furever Yours

The City Girl's Homecoming

This book is dedicated to the following people:

Laurita and Marc, who read every book.

My editor, Charles Griemsman, who worked
very hard to help make this book shine.

My husband and sons,
whose love and support sustain me.

Chapter One

How can you hate your best friend? Joni Danielson had pondered that question more times than she could count, and she still hadn't found a satisfactory answer. Nor had she discovered a way to rid herself of the negative feeling that had tormented her for the past six weeks. As she looked across the city hall conference room at Mayor Alexander Devlin III, her former friend, she was filled with anger and disappointment. And, truthfully, hate. And it hurt her heart. After five years of being best friends, she didn't want to hate him. But she didn't know how to stop.

For the past month and a half, she'd avoided being anyplace she thought he might show up. Since she knew him so well, she'd been successful most of the time. Once or twice she'd walked into Mabel's Diner and seen him there eating lunch and talking with people who came up to his table, but for the most part she'd steered clear of him. But some things, like this early-morning meeting with the city council and department heads, couldn't be avoided. Since she was director of the youth center in Sweet Briar, her presence was required.

Councilwoman Alana Kane swept into the room in a cloud of perfume that had Joni gagging. Despite the fact that it was seven thirty in the morning, the other woman's makeup was flawless, and there wasn't a hair out of place. Her earrings and necklace matched the diamond ankle bracelet on her left leg. She barely glanced at Joni as she strode across the room on four-inch heels. The smile she couldn't manage for Joni or any of the other people gathered in the room miraculously materialized when she reached Lex's side.

"Could she be any more transparent?"

Joni turned at the sound of Denise Harper's voice and met her eyes. Mrs. Harper was Lex's secretary, a position she'd held for several mayors before Lex. Joni considered the other woman a friend. "Only to us. You know men love getting all of a woman's attention, even if that woman is actually a snake in disguise."

"I thought Lex was smarter than that."

Joni frowned and, despite her determination not to, glanced over at Lex for a second, then back at Mrs. Harper. "He's not any more special than any other guy."

Mrs. Harper raised her eyebrows but otherwise didn't reply.

"Okay, it looks like everyone is here, so let's get this meeting started," Lex said. It seemed as if he sidestepped Alana, but that could be the way it appeared from Joni's perspective. And the smile on Alana's face never wavered as Joni imagined it would had she been ignored.

Joni headed for a chair near the foot of the table, but she was too slow, and one of the councilmembers beat her to it. Everyone else had taken a seat, and the only available chair was at Lex's right hand. In the past, she'd always sat there, so perhaps the other attendees were being courteous. Stifling a sigh, Joni took her seat and busied herself by searching for a pen in her purse.

Lex waited until everyone had taken a Danish or doughnut and topped up their coffee before calling the meeting to order. He glanced over at Joni, who held his gaze before she looked away. She recognized the question in his eyes, but she didn't understand why it was there. He knew what he'd done.

Lex picked up a typed sheet of paper. "Let's start with the first item on our agenda, the fall festival and dance."

These were new events that Lex had mentioned to Joni at breakfast months ago, back when they'd been best friends who'd spent endless hours together tossing ideas back and forth. Back before the incident that had changed everything.

They'd attended the wedding of one of her sorority sisters and pretended to be in love so Joni could save face in front of her cheating ex-fiancé and his wife, also one of Joni's sorority sisters. The plan had worked well until things got out of hand. She forced her mind away from that night. Besides, it wasn't that night that had ruined everything between them. Truth be told, the night she'd spent in Lex's arms had been the best of her life.

It was Lex's apology and remorse the next morning that had made remaining friends impossible. He'd gone on for ten minutes about how sorry he was, completely unaware of the joy that was seeping from her soul only to be replaced by regret and shame. And then anger had come. The shame and regret hadn't lasted long, but the anger and later hatred had grown stronger every day. At the time, she'd waited until he'd finally stopped saying they'd made a mistake, then gathered her clothes and gone into the bathroom where she'd showered and dressed in record time. Thankfully they'd been in a hotel in Chicago and not at home in Sweet Briar, North Carolina, where everyone would know what had transpired. At least no one would ever know how Lex had slept with her and then rejected her, saying they should pretend the whole night had never happened.

Joni forced the memory away and tuned back in to the meeting. And not a second too soon. That witch Alana was saying that since the dance would take place at the youth center, some of the money to pay for it should come from the youth center's budget. Joni held her tongue and her temper until the other woman finished speaking. Then Joni smiled and looked around at the other six councilmembers and the chief of police, Trent Knight, who was also in attendance. Finally she looked at Lex. "I'd like to address that if I might."

Lex nodded. "Go ahead."

"This is a function that will benefit the entire town, not just the youth, so it shouldn't come from our budget."

"The true focus is the kids, Jocelyn," Alana said snootily, using Joni's given name as opposed to her preferred nickname, a combination of her first and middle names. "The location is proof of that."

Joni managed to not roll her eyes. It was no secret that Alana wanted the dance to be held at a hotel in Charlotte that her brother managed. Charlotte was two hours away and holding the dance there would defeat the entire purpose. The fall festival was going to be a week-long promotional event where townspeople would try to convince vacationers that Sweet Briar was more than a beach town and summer destination. The plan was to let visitors see that Sweet Briar had plenty to offer all year round. The homecoming dance, which would be held a week after the festival, was meant to bring the town together for a good time after a week of hard but hopefully fruitful work.

Joni met and held Alana's gaze, speaking slowly and firmly. "It's for the families of Sweet Briar. The youth center is the logical choice because it has the most space."

"Regardless, if you're going to insist the dance take place at the center, the money should come from your budget. After all, the cost of security will be coming from the police budget."

"I see."

Alana nodded smugly. "I'm glad you agree."

"I don't agree. In fact, I think rather than charging the youth center, we should charge the city for use of our facility. After all, it will cost us in electricity and water usage. And of course janitorial. I'll call around to see what hotel and banquet halls charge to host similar functions and then send the city a bill."

Alana sputtered, and Joni managed not to smirk.

"The dance benefits the entire city, so it will come from our general budget," Lex said, putting an end to the matter. Not that Joni would have minded going a few more rounds with the other woman. The youth center did good work, and Joni would fight ferociously to protect every cent of her budget.

Alana frowned at Joni, then turned her attention back to Lex. She fluttered her obviously fake eyelashes. "I don't agree. Perhaps you'll give me a chance to change your mind later."

"There's no changing my mind. The decision is made. Now let's move on to the next matter."

They discussed other items on the agenda. Joni contributed where necessary, but otherwise she was more than happy to sit back and listen as others debated. Finally the meeting ended, and people began gathering their belongings. Most of the councilmembers had other jobs to get to, so they didn't linger after the meeting had been adjourned.

Not wanting to be alone with Lex, who was stacking his notes, Joni jumped to her feet and immediately felt nauseous and dizzy. She grabbed the back of the chair to steady herself. She'd overslept this morning and hadn't had time for even a quick breakfast. The pastries hadn't appealed to her, so she'd contented herself with a mug of coffee. That appeared to have been a mistake.

"Are you okay?"

Despite telling herself that she hated him, the unmistakable concern in Lex's voice had her biting back the caustic words gnawing at her insides. Being angry wasn't rational. She and Lex had both been willing participants that night. The fact that he'd had regrets the morning after didn't make him a bad person. Knowing that didn't lessen her anger, though. Emotions didn't listen to reason.

"I'm fine." She inhaled deeply and got a whiff of his enticing male scent. Lex's family had made their fortune in cosmetics and colognes, so naturally he always smelled good. She forced herself to stand up straight. "I missed breakfast. Once I eat something I'll be fine."

"Maybe you just need a little bit of sugar." He grabbed a jelly doughnut and offered it to her. She took one look, and her stomach lurched in rebellion. That greasy lump of dough oozing purple goo was the last thing she needed.

"No thanks. I'll get something decent at the diner." Truthfully the thought of food made her queasy, but not eating didn't seem to be doing her any favors, either.

"I'll drive you."

"That's not necessary. I have my car."

She started to walk away, but he placed a hand on her shoulder, stopping her progress. Her skin tingled where he touched her, and she stepped away. She needed to find her way back to the place where his touch didn't arouse longing in her. Back to where she'd been before they'd slept together.

"I don't mind taking you," he said. "I didn't eat, either. Maybe we can have breakfast together like we used to."

"I'm not staying. I'm calling in my order and taking it to go. I need to get to work."

Lex blew out a breath. Although his strong back was just as erect and his muscular shoulders were just as square as before, he seemed to sag. "Are you ever going to forgive me? I know I was wrong, and I'll apologize again if it makes a difference. I'm so sorry for what happened that night. I didn't mean to lose control like that. I miss our friendship. I miss hanging out together. I miss *you*."

Joni heard the naked pain in his voice, but she ignored it. She'd spent every night of the past six weeks missing him, too. But there was no going back. Their friendship had ended on a cloudy Sunday morning. She couldn't pretend that night hadn't happened the way he wanted her to. She couldn't bury her emotions. The hurt was real. Maybe one day it would be gone, but today wasn't that day. Maybe if she was more blasé about sex, she could chalk it up to a night of fun tangling in the sheets. But she couldn't. She wasn't made that way. Perhaps if she was a bigger person, she could accept his apology and they could be friends again. But the truth was, every time he apologized for making love to her—something she'd wanted—the hole he'd ripped in her heart tore a little bit more.

Fortunately she didn't have to respond. Alana, who'd been hanging around, had apparently gotten impatient and was now walking in their direction. Since Joni doubted the other woman wanted to speak to her, she picked up her purse. "Now isn't the time or the place to have a personal conversation. Besides, someone is waiting to talk to you. Maybe she can be your new best friend."

Joni turned to go, but not before she saw the exasperated expression that crossed Lex's face. She didn't know whether it was for her or for Alana. Who knew, maybe it was for both of them.

"This isn't over, Joni. I'll stop by later to talk."

Joni opened the door, then glanced over her shoulder. "I'm going to be busy."

He made a move in her direction, so she stepped through the door as quickly as possible. Though she'd won this round, Joni knew that Lex wouldn't give up easily. He'd be back, determined to continue the conversation, so she had to fortify herself. The first thing she needed to do was eat something. Hopefully she'd be able to keep it down this time.

Joni loved working at the youth center and spending time with kids and teenagers. Although she had administrative duties, she carved out a few hours each day to play with the little ones and talk to the older ones. Unfortunately that close contact left her susceptible to the illnesses kids brought with them. A stomach bug had run amok through the center for about a week. Several children had caught it, and a handful of volunteers had gotten sick as well. The kids bounced back in a day or two, but Derrick, one of the favorite youth leaders, had been sick for nearly a week.

Up until yesterday morning, Joni had believed she'd been one of the lucky ones who'd avoided getting sick. She'd awakened feeling nauseous, but she'd sipped a cup of green tea and nibbled on a slice of dry toast, and the feeling had passed. Now her stomach was lurching wildly, and she quickly changed her route from the parking lot to the ladies' restroom. She barely made it to a stall before she emptied the contents of her stomach.

When she was done, she stood and leaned her head against the door, waiting until the last of the nausea passed. She washed her hands, splashed water on her face and rinsed her mouth out. On most days she didn't bother with makeup, but staring at her reflection, her skin looked a bit pale. She rummaged through her purse, hoping to find a stray tube of lipstick that could give her some color. Unfortunately there was nothing there besides a month's worth of receipts and three crumpled napkins. She did find a pack of mints, so all wasn't lost.

Joni popped a mint into her mouth. Then feeling steadier, she left the bathroom and headed for her car. She hoped the stomach bug was the cause of her queasiness. Refusing to consider another reason for her upset stomach, she got into her car and drove the short distance to the diner. She'd only consider that other explanation when she couldn't avoid it any longer.

Lex watched as Joni fled the room, then swallowing his disappointment and annoyance, turned to deal with the councilwoman. She'd been elected to fill the seat of one of the old-time councilmembers who'd retired after the unexpected death of his wife. Lex had hoped that Alana would be a go-getter like the other new members whose fresh ideas had helped revitalize the town in the recent years. Though she'd only been on the council for three months, he'd already determined that she didn't share his vision for making Sweet Briar more prosperous. She had her own agenda, which involved enriching herself and her family. Lex had no problem with people making money. He and his family had made quite a lot of it over the years. But there was a difference between earning money in a private enterprise and using your elected position to take money from public coffers. He would never allow her to get rich by taking advantage of the citizens of Sweet Briar, whose interests he'd sworn to protect.

"What can I do for you?" Lex asked, keeping his voice professional yet cool.

"Let me take you to breakfast. I want the opportunity to convince you to move the ball to the hotel in Charlotte. I know my brother will give us a good deal. And it'll be a lot classier than a gym no matter how it's decorated."

"Thanks for the offer of breakfast, but I'll have to pass. And as far as the location for the dance goes, we already reached a decision with the full council present. I won't be changing my mind."

She stepped closer, putting a hand on his arm. "I can be very persuasive."

He took two steps away from her. "I don't operate that way. I don't make backroom deals, and I won't undercut my council."

The smile faded from her face. "I'm not trying to get you to undercut the council. I just want to make sure you have all of the facts before you make a final decision."

"I have all of the facts that you presented in the meeting. If there were more, you should have mentioned them in front of the entire council. It's too late now because everyone is gone. Not only that, the decision is final. Now, if there isn't anything else, I need to get back to work." He gestured for her to leave. She huffed out a breath and then, pulling the strap of her designer purse over her shoulder, stormed from the room. Hopefully that would be the end of her and this conversation, but he doubted it. She was probably planning on a second line of attack. He'd seen it all before and was immune.

He wanted to give her plenty of time to leave, so he straightened the conference room. The council-members had polished off the pastries, leaving behind only the doughnut Joni had rejected. Lex picked it up, scraped a handful of crumbs onto a paper plate, grabbed a couple of stray napkins, then tossed the entire mess into the trash. A cupful of coffee remained in the urn, so he poured it into a mug and headed down the hall to his office.

Mrs. Harper was already at her desk, typing. She smiled at him. "I saw Ms. Kane storm out of here. I take it that she wasn't happy with you when she left."

Denise Harper was a great secretary, and not simply because she kept his office running smoothly. More than being an extremely capable assistant, she could distinguish between a fake and the real thing in less time than it took to blink. She was also discreet, and he knew that whatever was said between them would be held in the strictest confidence.

"Not even a little bit. She might be used to manipulating people back in Charlotte, but I'm not going to be a pawn in her game. Someone must have misled her about the intelligence of small-town citizens."

"Or small-town mayors, at least."

He nodded. Alana really had thought she was playing him. If only she knew. He'd run into all sorts of vipers when he'd worked as a vice president in his family's company. Compared to them, she was a rank amateur. "She'll find out the truth soon enough."

"I also saw Joni leave."

Lex looked at his secretary. "How did she seem to you?"

She took her time before answering as if considering her words. "Something's off. I can't put my finger on what it is exactly, but she wasn't her usual self. But then, she might simply be sleepy. We did get an early start this morning."

"Maybe." Lex was an early riser by nature, and he liked to hit the ground running, but he knew Joni was the opposite. She preferred to ease into the day slowly, building up momentum as the morning progressed.

Not satisfied with that answer, but unable to come up with a better one of his own, Lex went to his office. He and Charlotte Tyler, Sweet Briar's manager of economic development, had been working hard to bring more businesses to town as well as investigating the feasibility of creating an arts center that would include a regional theater. He'd scheduled a meeting with her for that afternoon, so he reviewed the information she'd provided him in advance and made notes of questions he had.

Once that was done, he grabbed his cell phone and, after waving to Mrs. Harper, headed out the door. Every couple of days, he walked around town and talked to the citizens he encountered. Many people either couldn't attend public meetings or preferred not to. That didn't make their opinion any less valuable. It just meant he needed to find another way to communicate with them. These casual chats seemed to work. People who wouldn't feel comfortable visiting city hall didn't mind making a suggestion if they ran into him on the street. Lex enjoyed the conversations and looked forward to them.

He stopped to talk to a few men who were playing checkers in front of the barbershop. They were all retired and liked to congregate on nice days and chew the fat, as they called it. To a man, they claimed they were keeping an eye on the town as a sort of volunteer security force. Lex knew the truth. They were nosy and enjoyed gossiping. Although the four of them thought they had their fingers on the pulse of the town, they were usually the last to know about anything. Still, they were good company and often had creative suggestions for solving problems in the community.

"How's it going?" Lex asked as he reached the group. Mr. Harris was puffing on his pipe and studying the board. Lex dragged over an empty chair, then sat down. He glanced at the board. It didn't look good for Harold Wilson, a newly retired pharmacist who'd only recently joined the group.

"Fine if your name is Chester Harris," Wilbur Bolton said with a grin. "Not so fine if it's not."

The other men laughed, and Mr. Wilson shook his head. "That's a wrap. You can take my place if you want, Mayor."

"Not a chance," Lex said. "These guys are notorious for beating the unsuspecting."

"I was suspecting, and I still got my you-know-what handed to me."

Lex joined in the good-natured laughter.

"That's because you're a rookie," Mr. Harris said. "You'll get better after a while."

Lex talked to the men for a few more minutes before saying goodbye and continuing down the street. He stopped into several businesses and chatted with a few more people before he arrived at Mabel's Diner.

He'd spent more time than he'd planned conversing with people on the street, so the lunch crowd had come and gone by the time he arrived. Only a few tables were occupied.

Marla, a longtime waitress, was clearing a table. She looked up and smiled at him. "Take any seat, Mayor, and someone will be right with you."

He was about to tell her he wanted to get his food to go when the bell above the door chimed, signaling the arrival of a new patron. Glancing over his shoulder, he smiled. Joni. She walked to a booth near the front and took a seat before looking up. When she spied him, she paused and then looked away. He thought she might actually get up and leave. Could she really be that upset with him?

Once they'd been such good friends that he wouldn't have given joining her a second thought. Now, though, he hesitated. Would she be annoyed if he sat down with her, or did she also long for the days when they'd been close but just had no idea how to get that closeness back? Deciding that the best way to get things back to the way they'd been was to act normal, he crossed the diner and stood by her table. Instead of just sitting down, he paused. "Is it okay if I join you?"

For a second it seemed as if she wasn't going to answer. When she nodded, he slid into the booth, across from her. She picked up her menu as if studying it, but he knew better. The diner had been serving the same meals for the entire time he'd lived in Sweet Briar. He understood from residents who lived here when the diner first opened nearly forty years ago that very little had changed. It didn't take a genius to know that Joni wasn't interested in having a conversation. He wouldn't push her to talk. He was just glad she willingly let him be in her presence.

Peggy, the waitress, came up to the table, pad in hand. "I haven't seen the two of you together in a while. What can I get for you?"

Joni put down the menu. "I'll have half a turkey sandwich, a cup of chicken and rice soup and a glass of ginger ale."

That was different. Most days she got a burger and fries, same as him. Perhaps she was trying something new. Or maybe she didn't feel well. She'd once told him that her mother had made her drink ginger ale whenever she'd been sick as a child and that she associated the beverage with illness. He placed his usual order and then studied Joni surreptitiously.

It wasn't exaggerating to say that she was the most beautiful woman he'd ever laid eyes on. With rich brown eyes, high cheekbones and clear brown skin, she had the face of an angel. Her wavy black hair reached to the middle of her back. Most days she wore a headband that held it off her face, but today it bounced freely around her shoulders. About five foot seven and built like a model, she had the grace of a ballerina.

Although she looked good dressed in the casual clothes she wore to work at the youth center, she looked stunning when she dressed up. He'd lost his breath when he'd seen her in her bridesmaid's dress six weeks ago. And later that night he'd lost control, something that filled him with guilt and remorse whenever he thought about it. Not that he regretted making love with her. He could never regret that. But he hated the way that one night had destroyed their friendship. He'd apologized right away, but the damage had been done. He was still searching for a way to undo it.

Looking at her now, her skin didn't possess its usual glow. And her eyes didn't sparkle the way they did on most days. Maybe the strain on their friendship was affecting her physically. If that was the case, she wasn't alone. He wasn't sleeping well and spent most nights tossing and turning. There was disquiet in his spirit, and the only way to get rid of it was to get their relationship back on track. He might be wrong, but he thought Joni's issues might be related. Perhaps they both needed to get back to normal in order to feel better.

"How are things at the center?" he asked.

She sighed and finally looked straight at him. "Busy. Now that school is out, we're bursting at the seams. Not that I'm complaining. I prefer having the kids at the center to leaving them to their own devices. I have a lot of things planned for the summer."

"Like what?"

She smiled and leaned against the back of the booth and began to go into detail about her latest plans. As she talked, her shoulders relaxed, and she once more was the woman he'd known so well. They'd hit it off from the moment they'd met nearly five years ago, becoming fast friends. Before long they were spending most of their free time together. Now that she was angry at him, he was left with time on his hands. Even after six weeks, he was still amazed by how deeply it hurt not having her around and how much he missed her.

While they ate, Lex noted with relief that the color returned to Joni's skin. Perhaps ginger ale did contain medicinal properties after all. More importantly, the tension between them that had been an unwanted third wheel had eased a bit. Lex didn't delude himself into believing all was right between them now. It would take more than one lunch to do that. But he was committed to becoming close friends again. He just needed a chance.

Chapter Two

"What are you doing Friday?"

Joni swallowed the last of her ginger ale and placed the empty glass on the table. She'd managed to eat all of her lunch and finally felt human again. Not only that, for the first time in weeks she felt comfortable with Lex. It was as if the night they'd spent together and the horribly embarrassing morning after hadn't happened. But it had happened, and she couldn't allow herself to pretend otherwise. To do so would only cause more problems and bring her more pain. Sadly there was no going back for her and Lex. Their friendship had been damaged much too badly for that.

Perhaps she wasn't as nice a person as she'd believed. Maybe a nicer person would get over her hurt and move on from here as if nothing had happened. But that would leave her vulnerable, and she was determined to protect her heart this time. This wasn't the first time a man had taken all she had to give and then rejected her. And though he may not acknowledge it, Lex had rejected her. He hadn't been as rude and cruel as Darrin had been when he'd told her that he no longer loved her and then asked for his engagement ring back. He hadn't let her absorb that shock before saying that he'd been seeing one of her sorority sisters behind her back. Oh and by the way, he intended to marry Trina instead of Joni.

No, Lex had simply emphasized that sleeping with Joni had been a mistake—one that he had no intention of making again. Surely he had to know how deeply that had hurt her. They'd been friends long enough for him to know that she didn't take sex lightly. He had to have been aware that she would never have slept with him if she didn't care about him a great deal. Apparently they didn't know each other as well as she'd thought they had, because Lex hadn't understood any of that. He had no clue what she'd been feeling then or what she felt now.

Here he sat, staring at her with those gorgeous brown eyes, rubbing the neatly trimmed hair of his beard and waiting for her to fall back into their pattern of spending all of their spare time together. She'd spent the past six weeks binge-watching TV and eating endless pints of Ben & Jerry's Chocolate Therapy ice cream. Though she'd missed his running commentary on the shows she watched almost as much as she missed falling asleep on his shoulder, she wasn't going to slip back into that habit. She'd get over it eventually. Even so, it was hard to force out the words. "I have plans."

The disappointment that snatched away his hopeful, dimpled smile was like a dart to her heart. She wouldn't weaken, though. She needed to consider her own feelings. He'd be fine without her. After all, Alana was lurking in the background, ready to provide Lex with whatever he wanted. All he had to do was ask.

Lex beckoned Peggy, who immediately brought over their checks. He took both and handed her several bills before Joni had a chance to move. "Keep the change."

The waitress glanced at the money in her hand and then flashed him a broad smile. "Thanks, Mayor. I hope you both have a great day."

"I could have paid for my own lunch," Joni said as she stood.

"I know." Lex jumped to his feet. His ingrained manners wouldn't allow him to remain seated. "You can pay next time."

She sputtered. While she was searching for the words to let him know there would be no next time, he continued talking.

"I've got a meeting in a few minutes. See you later."

Not if I see you first. Unable to stop herself, she watched as he left the diner. It was okay to admire his muscular physique from a distance. As long as she didn't get confused and allow herself to get swept away by her overactive imagination and start believing they had a future together, she could look all she wanted.

Before returning to the youth center, Joni made a detour to Louanne's Homemade Candy and ordered a pound of chocolate-covered almonds. After a second's hesitation, she added a pound of chocolate-covered pretzels.

"It must be some kind of day," Louanne said as she measured the chocolate on the scale, dropping the last few nuts one at a time until the arrow pointed at one pound. "Or maybe that time of the month."

"I just had a taste for chocolate," Joni said. Ordinarily she would engage in conversation, but Lex's comments had left her rattled. He'd been making it plain that he wasn't going to vanish from her life.

"Okay," the other woman said dubiously as she slid the almonds into a white paper bag and folded it closed. She weighed and packaged the pretzels as expertly, handed them to Joni, then rang up the order on an old-fashioned cash register. Joni handed over some money and, exercising great self-control, tucked the bags into her purse. The chocolate was a treat to be eaten later tonight when she was alone at home. But now it was time to get back to work.

When Joni pulled up to the center, she looked at the vibrant mural on the outside of the building. It had been created by Joni's good friend, Carmen Knight, and painted by kids and volunteers. The art always lifted Joni's spirits and reminded her of how far the youth center had come in a relatively short time. How much good they had done.

When Joni had moved to Sweet Briar from Chicago almost five years ago, the youth center had been in its infancy and run only by volunteers. The building had been plain gray on the outside. The inside had been a maze of rooms with basic white walls. She'd immediately recognized the potential in the blank canvas she'd been handed and set out to utilize it in ways that would benefit the children. Her experience as a social worker in Chicago had given her the insight into the kinds of programs young people needed to help them grow into happy and productive adults.

It had taken a lot of time and hard work—both hers and that of volunteers—to turn the youth center into what it was now. They provided services not only to the children who lived in town, but to those who lived in the surrounding areas as well. No child who wanted to participate in youth center activities was turned away. Last year she'd had the funds to hire two full-time employees—Analisa, her assistant director, and Bonita, a cook. But Joni wasn't resting on her laurels. She had bigger dreams of the services the center would provide to a larger number of kids in a greater area.

After stowing her purse in her office, she visited the various rooms to check on the kids. She stopped by the computer lab and the gym, two of the busiest areas, and talked with the kids. A lot of the kids were on the playground, so Joni hung out with them for a while before continuing her rounds. The last room she visited was the art room. Carmen headed up the department, but with twin toddlers, she didn't spend as much time at the center as she had in the past. She was there today, and Joni stepped in for a chat.

"Hey," Carmen said. The seven- and eight-year-olds had completed their projects, and Carmen was wiping tables as she set up the room for the next group of kids who'd be arriving in fifteen minutes. The little kids loved painting, but just as much paint landed on the surfaces all around the room as on their projects.

"How's it going?"

"Crazy as usual. Thankfully Joseph is home from college and helping a couple of days a week when he's not at work. He's a godsend."

Joseph had attended the youth center as a high-school student. It warmed Joni's heart whenever one of the kids who'd benefited from the center returned to volunteer. It validated her belief that they were positively affecting young lives and serving the community. "How are your kids?"

Carmen had married Trent, a widowed father of two daughters, and they'd had the twin boys together.

"Busy. Alyssa has a part-time job at Hannah's boutique. Even though she's not much into fashion, she enjoys working there. Robyn's jealous because she wants a real job now. Getting paid to watch the boys has lost its thrill. Working around designer clothes would be my little fashion plate's dream job."

Joni laughed. "And my godsons?"

"They're hanging around with the other kids in the playroom. And I know they would love a hug from their godmother."

"I'll be sure to give them one." Joni loved Carmen's kids, but lately when she was around them, she felt a strange yearning for a kid of her own. Of course she would need a man for that. If the past was a predictor of the future, the odds weren't in her favor.

Joni had always considered herself to have led a charmed life. She had a loving and supportive family. She had a job she loved and good friends. Unfortunately her luck ran out before it reached the romance department. First there'd been a broken engagement. It had taken her a while, but she'd finally gotten over that betrayal. Now there was Lex's rejection. Just thinking about that morning made her heart ache, yet she hadn't found a way to keep the memories away. She knew no good could come from thinking about that day. It was over and done, as was their friendship. Not only that, she was giving up on romance once and for all, so she would just have to content herself with the kids at the youth center.

"What do you think?"

Joni looked at Carmen's face. "I'm sorry, what did you say?"

"I just invited you over for dinner."

"Sure that would be great. Just let me know when. We'd better get these tables done." She glanced around. All of them were clean and ready to go. Just how long had she been daydreaming? She looked at the sponge in her hand. It had dripped water all over the table.

"Are you okay?" Carmen asked. "You seem sort of spacey."

Joni quickly dried the mess. "I'm fine. I just have something on my mind."

"Okay. I'm always available to listen."

"I'll keep that in mind," Joni said, edging toward the door. She wasn't ready to talk yet, but she didn't want to hurt Carmen's feelings by shutting her out.

"Can we come in now?" a little girl with pigtails asked.

"Sure," Carmen said.

Saved. Joni greeted the kids, then dashed from the room. She knew her behavior had raised Carmen's suspicion, but it couldn't be helped.

Lex closed his car door, then waved at a family as they drove out of the youth-center parking lot. It had been three days since he'd seen Joni but it seemed longer.

The center was quieting down as most of the kids

had been picked up and were on their way home for the night. However, there was a group waiting for him. He had a standing arrangement with the teenage boys for a few games of basketball, followed by pizza.

He'd started playing with the boys several years ago in order to develop a better relationship with them than the previous mayor had. To Lex, everyone in Sweet Briar was important. From the oldest senior citizen to the youngest infant, Lex was determined to serve them all. But he couldn't address their concerns if he didn't know what they were. The older people were more inclined to attend meetings or stop him on the street to talk. The youth didn't do either of those things. So he met them on their territory and built relationships so they would feel comfortable with him.

When he'd started coming to the youth center, the youngest kids welcomed him with open arms. They didn't care that he was the mayor. To them he was one more person to ooh and aah over their artwork; one more person to attend their pageants and cheer at their sporting events.

The teens had been suspicious of his motives and slow to accept him. It had taken a while, but he'd won their trust. Several of them had begun to take an active part in his initiatives around town. They'd even approached him with ideas, a couple of which he'd implemented. No matter what else was going on in his life, he didn't miss his Thursday-night basketball game. Given his troubles with Joni, the games had become the highlight of his week.

When he'd first organized the game, he'd required the chief of police to join as well. Lex believed that a good relationship between the youth and law enforcement was essential. Soon local business owners and fathers had joined, and now adult vs. teen games were held three nights a week. But basketball wasn't for everyone, so some teens and adults had formed a bowling league and made weekly trips to nearby Willow Creek for games. Lex was hoping to entice someone with an entrepreneurial mind to reopen the old Sweet Briar Lanes and was currently meeting with an interested couple. If that didn't pan out, he'd talk to Joni about joining him in a campaign to raise funds to build a four-lane alley at the youth center.

Thoughts of Joni had him pausing. He'd picked up his phone to call her several times over the past few days and had even contemplated driving past her house, but hadn't. That seemed a bit stalkerish even to him. If she wanted some distance from him, the right thing to do was give it to her. But how much space did she need or want? And how much was too much? When would the space she wanted turn into an uncrossable chasm? He'd misjudged the difference with a woman once, and it had cost him his marriage.

He'd lost his wife's love by giving her the time she'd asked for after their infant daughter's sudden death. Though he'd been heartbroken himself, he'd tried to comfort Caroline. No matter what he tried, he hadn't been able to reach her. She'd asked for space, and he'd given it to her. She'd put up walls, and he'd foolishly let them remain. He'd hoped that she would return to him after she'd grieved, so he'd left her to mourn on her own while he'd buried himself in work. At the time he'd been an executive vice president at his family's cosmetic and perfume business and traveled frequently. One day when he'd come back from an overseas trip, Caroline told him she didn't love him any longer and wanted a divorce. Blindsided, he'd tried to talk her out of it. When she'd insisted that she wanted her freedom—needed it in order to be happy again—he'd given it to her. The last thing he wanted to do was imprison her in a marriage she didn't want. He'd loved her enough to let her go so that she could find happiness.

A few months later, with his parents' and siblings' blessing, he'd quit his job and moved to Sweet Briar, North Carolina. He'd visited Sweet Briar once years ago and hadn't forgotten the people he'd met in the struggling town. They'd been kind and welcoming, despite the fact that the town was slowly going under.

The previous mayor and town council had either not cared or been too incompetent to help the people, so Lex had filled the void. He'd started small, making recommendations to business owners and helping where he could. Frustrated by the lack of political will he sensed in the leadership, he'd run for mayor and won. He'd thrown his heart and soul into helping the dying town to come alive again. It had taken hard work and dedication, but Sweet Briar was now a thriving town. He'd run unopposed in last year's election, proof that he was doing something right.

If only he could manage to get things right in his personal life.

He brushed that thought aside and continued to the gym. He was nearly there when he spotted someone rushing to the bathroom. In a flash he recognized Joni. Recalling how ill she'd appeared earlier in the week, he turned around and went to stand outside the women's restroom. If she was sick, he wanted to be there to offer his assistance. She might not feel well enough to drive home. The sound of retching reached his ears followed by a long silence. He was contemplating knocking on the door when it swung open.

"Lex. What are you doing?"

"Checking up on you."

"Why?" She folded her arms across her chest and leaned against the doorjamb. He stared at her, trying to determine if she was using the doorframe for support or if she was just irritated. Her skin had a decidedly green tinge to it, and she was sucking on a mint like it was giving her life. Was she sick? He spent enough time at the center to know that several of the kids had been sick recently. They'd bounced right back, so even if Joni had caught the bug, it wasn't anything serious. Still, the idea of her having even a minor illness unnerved him.

"I saw you rushing in here and was concerned."

"I'm fine. Now, if you don't mind, I'm ready to go home. It's been a long day."

He stepped aside immediately. What else could he do? Clearly she wasn't going to take him into her confidence. Nor was she inviting him to stop by after the game as she had so many times in the past. "Have a good evening."

She nodded but otherwise didn't reply.

As he watched her go, he felt compelled to call after her. "I'm here if you need me."

"I won't."

Telling himself she didn't mean the words the way they sounded, he went to the gym. The teens were already warming up, making layups with ease. A few teenage girls were seated in the bleachers, no doubt waiting for the game to start.

"Hey. I was worried that you'd backed out."

Lex dropped his bag on a chair, then looked over at Trent Knight, the chief of police and his closest friend. "Nah. I stopped to talk to Joni for a minute."

"Is she coming to watch?"

"No. She's going home." He managed to keep the disappointment from his voice.

"Then I guess I only have to worry about the teenagers showboating."

"What's that supposed to mean? I never showboat."

"You're kidding, right?" Rick Tyler, the town's doctor and one of the newest members of the team, said as he joined them. "You act like you're trying out for the NBA whenever Joni's around. You fly around the court like you're sixteen. Before you try to deny it, remember I have the medical records to prove it."

"That was one time. I landed wrong and twisted my ankle."

"Only because you were hanging from the basket with one hand, trying to impress a certain woman," Trent said.

"And don't forget how he nearly dislocated his shoulder swatting the ball away from your future son-in-law," Rick said to Trent.

Trent held up his hands. "Don't even play like that. Alyssa is too young to think about getting married to Joseph or anyone else."

The other men laughed and, though his heart ached, Lex joined them.

"Are you guys ready?" Jeremy, one of the teenagers, called.

Lex glanced over his shoulder. The teens had finished warming up and were watching the men with a mixture of amusement and impatience. "Yeah. Get ready to lose big-time."

The teens glanced at each other and laughed raucously. Although it had been agreed that the games were only good fun, everyone knew the record. The teens had beaten the adults in nearly two-thirds of the games they'd played. Most by double digits.

"You should wait until you're home in bed before you start dreaming," Jeremy said. The other teens laughed again.

Tonight there were eight youths and nine adults. That meant his team had a fighting chance to win one of the three games, although Lex didn't hold out much hope. Not with the pretty teenage girls providing extra motivation for the other team. It didn't help that the adult team included two players built for football. They were solid as walls but couldn't jump an inch and were slow. A third player was better suited for working the concession stand. Reminding himself that the game was supposed to be purely recreational, Lex went in for the jump ball, which he won.

As the teams raced up and down the floor, Lex managed to channel some of his frustration with Joni into the game. He and his team played hard, but the teenagers had youth on their side. At halftime the adults were down by twelve points. Lex's team took the six-minute break to guzzle sports drinks and try to catch their breath. The teens chose to horse around or flirt with the girls.

"So what's up with Joni?" Trent asked quietly.

Lex looked around. The rest of their team was

sprawled on benches too far away to listen in on the conversation. "What do you mean?"

"Carmen mentioned that Joni was acting a little bit strange the past couple of days."

"In what way?"

"She didn't say. I talked to Joni myself for a couple of minutes, and she seemed a little bit off. Maybe she was tired or didn't feel well." Trent shrugged. "It might sound crazy, but she reminded me of Carmen when she was pregnant. A little distracted, a little emotional. But then, she is handling a lot here at the center, so there was probably another reason she wasn't herself. Forget I said anything."

That was easier said than done. The whistle blew, signaling the end of halftime. Still, Trent's words echoed in Lex's head. Could Joni be pregnant? And if she was, did she plan on telling him? He told himself to slow down and stop jumping to conclusions. Joni might actually just be ill. But there was only one way to find out. He was going to have to ask her. He knew he'd promised to give her space, but he'd drive himself insane wondering if she was going to have a baby.

Joni dropped the pregnancy test into the garbage can and then sank onto the side of the tub. Positive. She'd known that was going to be the case. She had avoided thinking about the possibility of a baby for as long as she could. But after being sick for the past three days, she'd decided it was time to face the truth, whatever it was. Once she'd gotten out her calendar and checked for the date of her last period, she'd been all but certain she was pregnant. Joni was one of those rare women who was regular. Every thirty days, down to the hour, like-clockwork regular. And she was late. Combined with her nausea and sudden desire to sleep, she'd known she was pregnant. But ever cautious—and hopeful—she'd taken a break this afternoon, driven to Walmart out on the highway, and purchased every brand of pregnancy test they sold. When she'd gotten home, she'd headed for the bathroom and one by one she'd used them. Not one had come back negative. The latest positive only confirmed what she'd discovered an hour ago.

What was she going to do? The quick and easy answer was have a baby. She knew that. In under eight months she was going to give birth to a son or daughter. The thought, scary as it was, also made her heart skip with joy. She could practically feel the warm bundle squirming in her arms. She'd always planned on being a mother. Of course, in her vision she'd had a loving and supportive husband beside her, sharing her happiness. Her imaginary husband had yet to materialize. Instead she'd become pregnant by a man whose first words the morning after they'd made love were that they'd made a mistake. Not what she'd wanted to hear and definitely not anything that gave her hope of a shared future. At least, not the future she'd pictured having with her child's father.

Lex wanted to be friends. Pals. He wanted to keep her at a distance while he dated and perhaps fell in love with another woman. Maybe that horrible Alana Kane had already gotten her claws into him. Not that Joni could allow herself to care. She'd driven down that road once before after her former fiancé had dumped her. Heartbroken, Joni had tried to figure out what she'd done wrong in order to make it right. It had taken her a long time to realize that she hadn't done anything wrong. He'd been the one lying and cheating. Looking back at her behavior, the only excuse she had was that she'd been so much younger and naïve then. And foolish. Well, she was neither of those things now.

She lifted her hair off her neck, then let it fall over her shoulders. Her decision to keep Lex out of her life needed to be revisited. There was no way she would be able to do that once she'd given birth. Lex might not want her in his life, but she knew he wasn't the type to run away from his responsibilities. Not only that, he loved kids just as much as she did. More than once she'd seen the longing on Lex's face when he was around the little kids, the yearning in his eyes when he drank imaginary beverages at one of the endless tea parties the four- and five-year-olds loved to have. The paternal patience he displayed, as he showed a boy how to knot a tie or told him how to know if a girl really liked him, had warmed Joni's heart. Without a doubt Lex would make a great father.

The biggest problem she could foresee was how she would deal with him. Raising a child would require the two of them to work together. She wanted her child to know that even though his parents weren't married, they could get along. That meant she would have to find a way to stop being angry at Lex. It wouldn't be easy, but she was going to have to get her feelings under control. Undoubtedly Lex would date in the future, so she was going to have to come to grips with seeing him with another woman after he'd dumped her so easily.

Her heart ached at the thought. She inhaled deeply, then slowly blew out the breath. Lex's potential romances were not something she wanted to contemplate right now. Given the fact that she was still trying to accept that she'd become pregnant from what amounted to a one-night stand, she was entitled to avoid anything unsettling. Joni knew she would have to face reality at some point. And she was going to have to tell Lex she was pregnant. But she didn't have to do either of those things right now. She wouldn't be showing for at least two more months. And if she dressed carefully, she might be able to camouflage her pregnancy for a month past that, giving herself more time to adjust.

One thing was certain. She wasn't ready to tell Lex about the baby. She needed time to come to grips with it herself, first. For the time being, her pregnancy would be her very own secret. That decided, she washed her hands and went into the kitchen.

When she'd moved to Sweet Briar, she'd shared a house with her brother, Brandon. He was a fabulous chef and owned the best restaurant in a three-state area. When he'd fallen in love with and married one of his waitresses, Joni had moved from the house into the garage apartment. She liked the privacy it afforded while still allowing her to be close to Brandon and Arden, her sister-in-law. As she looked around the cozy apartment, she realized that it was a one-person home. It definitely didn't have enough room for a kid to run and play. Of course, since the baby wasn't even as big as her thumb and wouldn't be making an appearance for months, she had time to find a house of her own with all the space they would need.

She was warming up food she'd picked up from Brandon's restaurant on the way home from work when someone knocked on her door. It was not quite nine o'clock, so Brandon and Arden would still be at the restaurant. Sighing, she crossed the small room and peered through her peephole.

Lex. What was he doing here? Her heart thudded in her chest, and for a moment she froze. She briefly considered pretending not to be home, but she knew he'd never be fooled.

"I can hear you moving around in there," he said, confirming Joni's thought.

She unlocked the door and swung it open. He was dressed in a navy T-shirt and gray basketball shorts. No doubt he'd come straight from the youth center after the Thursday games. For a moment she wondered if there'd been a problem, but she shut down that thought immediately. How big a problem could there be with both the mayor and the chief of police present? And if there had been a medical emergency, the town doctor would have been there to help. No, Lex was here for personal reasons.

"What do you want?"

"To talk."

"About?" Joni knew she was stalling, but her mind couldn't quite function.

"Us."

"There is no *us*." She started to close the door, but he grabbed it and held it open. Irritated, she looked into his face. The determination she saw in his eyes made her tremble.

"Are you pregnant?"

Chapter Three

The color drained from Joni's face, and Lex mentally kicked himself. He hadn't meant to blurt out his question that way, but when he saw the door closing, he'd panicked. He wanted to talk as one adult to another, but he'd seen his opportunity vanishing and didn't know when he'd get another one. He touched her shoulder. "I didn't mean to be so abrupt, but my question remains. Are you pregnant?"

Joni didn't answer right away, but she did open the door wider. "Come on in."

Lex stepped inside and then took a seat on the sofa. Despite the serious conversation that they were about to have, some of the tension eased from his body the moment he stepped into the apartment. He'd spent so many pleasant hours here that it felt like he'd come home. Deciding to let Joni take the conversational lead, he sat back and crossed his feet at the ankles, doing his best to disguise his nerves. Ever since Trent had said the word *pregnant*, Lex had been on pins and needles, his stomach churning nonstop. The idea had taken root, and no matter how he'd tried to shake it off while he played ball, he couldn't.

Joni sat in a chair across from him, and Lex found his eyes drawn to her abdomen. It was still as flat as ever, not that he'd expected any different. There was no reason she would be showing at six weeks. Still, he couldn't keep from picturing her belly large with his child. That is, if she was actually pregnant.

Joni tapped her fingertips together, a sign that she was nervous. "I only did the test a little while ago."

"And?" he asked when she only sat there staring into space.

She looked straight in his eyes. When she spoke, her voice was barely over a whisper, and it shook. "Yes. I'm pregnant."

Despite being prepared to hear the words, his heart still stuttered when she actually said them. Joni was pregnant. They'd made a child together. Conflicting emotions battered him on every side. Years ago when his little girl had been born, he'd been ecstatic. He'd loved her beyond words and sometimes more than his heart could contain. He'd had so many plans for her future. He was going to give her the world.

Then, without warning, at four weeks and three days of age, Briana had died. He'd been gutted. Nothing had ever hurt as much as seeing his little angel lying in a tiny casket. He'd wanted to die, too. A father was supposed to protect his child, and he'd failed. After his daughter's death, he'd been unwilling to open his heart like that again, which was why he'd always been so careful about birth control. He couldn't risk getting a woman pregnant and bringing another child into the world. But a few weeks ago, he'd slipped up, and now Joni was pregnant.

"Say something." Joni's voice reeked of desperation, a sound he'd never wanted to hear from her.

"I don't know what to say." Though he'd never wanted to be vulnerable to that type of loss again and fear was currently gripping his soul, he couldn't deny the bit of hope and joy that was struggling to come alive inside him. He had a second chance to be a father. This time he would be more careful. Although the doctors insisted there was nothing he or Caroline could have done to prevent Briana from dying, a part of his parental heart believed he was to blame.

"I'm keeping it." Though her voice trembled, her words were defiant.

His heart nearly stopped at her words. Had that been in doubt? And in that moment, all ambivalence vanished. He wanted this baby. "I hope you know I would never try to convince you otherwise."

Joni's eyebrows eased, and her shoulders relaxed. Apparently she'd been prepared for a battle. "I just wanted to make that plain from the beginning. And I also want to let you know that I didn't get pregnant on purpose."

"I know that, Joni. I was there." He remembered every blissful second of their night together. It had been one of the best nights of his life. And it had cost him the most important relationship in his life. If he could go back in time, he'd do everything differently. He wouldn't agree to be Joni's pretend boyfriend at her sorority sister's wedding. He still would have gone to Chicago with her, but as the friend that he'd actually been. Acting like they were in love had led to some very real kisses and caresses that had landed them in this situation. She was barely speaking to him. All because he'd betrayed her friendship.

After his marriage had fallen apart, he'd tried to love again. More than once he'd made an effort to let a woman get close. But he couldn't. The part of his heart responsible for becoming a good mate had died. He wasn't able to open himself up like that anymore. Not that he'd been a monk. Not even close. But he'd always made sure that the woman he was involved with knew he wasn't offering forever. Forever was no longer an option for him. Neither was love. All he had to offer was respect, kindness and faithfulness for however long the relationship lasted. And the women had been fine with that because they hadn't been looking for anything permanent, either.

But Joni was different. He'd recognized that early in their friendship. She would never be satisfied with the little he'd been able to give. She wanted everything. They'd discussed their hopes for the future on more than one occasion. She wanted a husband and kids, a forever love like her parents shared. She deserved to have what she wanted. At one time he'd considered introducing her to one of his younger brothers who'd be able to give her the family she wanted. Somehow he'd never gotten around to doing that. Now it was too late.

Though Lex had tried to put things back the way they'd been the morning after he and Joni had made love by apologizing and suggesting they pretend that nothing had happened, it hadn't worked. The easy comfort they'd shared was gone, and no matter how hard he tried, he couldn't get it back. He was trying to become her friend again, but she wasn't interested. Still, he'd held out hope that he could win her over eventually.

Now that she was pregnant, there was no way they could pretend that night hadn't happened and go back to being best friends. The child would be proof that for at least one night they'd been lovers. Unfortunately he didn't know what kind of relationship they could have in the future. If he couldn't convince her to be his friend again… He couldn't imagine that. He had to find a way to win her back. She'd liked him once. She could like him once again.

"I'm still trying to wrap my mind around the fact that I'm going to have a baby and figure out what to do next."

"What do you want to do?"

She shrugged. "I have no clue. It's all kind of surreal. This isn't at all how I'd planned it. I always thought I'd be married when I had a baby. I'm kind of traditional that way. And then there's my job. As director of the youth center, I'm supposed to be setting an example for the younger generation."

"You're doing a fantastic job and you know it."

"By getting pregnant after a one-night stand?"

He reared back. Her words might as well have been a fist. "The night we shared might not have been planned or repeated, but it definitely wasn't a *one-night stand.*"

"Then, what would you call it? Besides a *mistake*, I mean."

"I don't know. Two friends who got swept up by the pretense and slipped up?"

She shook her head and laughed. It wasn't a joyous sound. It took a moment before he realized that tears were sliding down her face. He jumped off the couch and knelt in front of her chair. He cupped her face, angling it so that their eyes met. The pain he saw in hers was nearly his undoing. The last thing he'd ever wanted to do was hurt her. "It's going to be all right. Everything is going to be okay. I promise."

"No, it won't. Nothing will ever be okay again."

"It only seems like that now because everything is turned upside down. You've gotten a shock. You're still trying to deal with it. We both are. But we'll handle it together. Okay?"

"I can't."

"Can't what?"

"Handle this with you. Not this. Not now."

"Why not?"

"Because I—I don't like you anymore."

"I see."

Joni watched wordlessly as Lex pushed to his feet. He didn't return to the couch, but went to her front door. For one tense minute she thought he might leave, but he didn't. Instead he leaned against the wall and crossed his arms over his chest. Despite the fact that she didn't want to be attracted to him, she couldn't help but notice the way his shirt pulled tight against his muscular torso. Even though Lex's job required him to do a lot of sitting, and frequently involved lunch or dinner meetings, he possessed a spectacular body without an ounce of flab. Every inch of his six-foot-three-inch frame was perfectly sculpted.

She dragged her eyes away from his body and her mind away from the memory of running her hands over his chest and six-pack abs. That was something that would never be repeated and therefore was best forgotten. She forced herself to focus on the conversation. "I'm not trying to hurt your feelings, Lex. I'm just being honest. That night changed things for me in more ways than one. I can't pretend nothing happened the way you want to and go back to the way things were."

"So what are you suggesting we do? Because I can tell you right now I'm not going to walk away from my child."

"What makes you so sure it's yours?" She was bluffing, of course. She hadn't dated anyone in longer than she cared to think about and hadn't had sex with anyone other than Lex for even longer. Several guys had asked her out, but after a few horrible first dates she'd opted to spend her free time with Lex. Being with him had been a lot more enjoyable than those awkward dates. To be honest, being with him had been a lot more fun than anything.

He laughed. "That's probably the only thing I'm sure of right now."

She had to smile. "Me too."

"I think we both need time to think about this. How about we table this discussion and meet for lunch tomorrow? Our heads will be clearer then."

"I don't think that's a good idea. What I really need is time and space alone."

"I'm not asking you to move in with me, Joni. All I'm asking is for us to have lunch and talk. And you know you need to eat. Now that you're pregnant, you can't skip meals the way you did the other day."

"I can always go over to Brandon and Arden's. My brother is a chef, you know. And he's close by."

Lex raised an eyebrow. He didn't say a word, but then he didn't need to. They knew each other so well that silent communication was just as effective as words. He knew that although she lived in the garage apartment behind her brother and sister-in-law's Victorian home, she didn't like to intrude on their privacy. After all, they were newlyweds.

Joni sighed. "Okay. I'll meet you at the diner."

"Good. Usual time?"

Joni nodded and stood up. Lex didn't say anything else, but she could tell there was more on his mind. In the old days, she would have prodded him to talk, but this wasn't the old days. And who knew, perhaps it was better that he kept it to himself for the moment. She didn't have the emotional space to deal with anything else.

Happy that she was able to stand without feeling the tiniest bit of nausea, Joni crossed the room to open the door for him. She expected him to move out of her way, but he didn't. Instead he put his hand under her chin and lifted her face until their eyes met. The warmth and concern she saw there didn't surprise her. Lex had always been a caring person. What surprised her was the sudden longing that filled her.

If someone had told her two months ago that Lex's simplest touch would set her on fire, she would have laughed that person out of town. She'd known Lex possessed a lethal charm and magnetism that women found irresistible, but she'd believed herself to be immune. She couldn't count the number of occasions they'd sat on her sofa, her feet on his lap. Or the many times he'd thrown his arm over her shoulder and pulled her against his strong side. Not once had her knees weakened. She hadn't felt a spark of anything resembling attraction. Now, though, his slightest touch awakened parts of her body that had lain dormant for years until that night six weeks ago. Somehow she had to get them to go back to sleep. At least where Lex was concerned.

"I'll see you tomorrow."

"Okay." She hated the breathless sound to her voice, so she cleared her throat and then stepped away from him. Still he didn't leave. "Did you want something else?"

"Have you eaten anything?"

"I stopped by Heaven on Earth and picked up dinner. I was just heating it up when you got here."

That seemed to satisfy him. "Okay, then. Sleep well."

He opened the door and descended the stairs with the ease of a man without a care in the world. Joni watched until he climbed into his car and drove away before she closed the door. Unable to move, she leaned against it and exhaled. That had gone better than she'd expected. And even though she hadn't wanted to tell Lex about the baby yet, she was glad to have the discussion out of the way. She didn't like keeping secrets from him. That was something they'd never done in the past. And even though their relationship had changed for the worse and everything else between them was different, it was good to know that at least one thing was the same.

She reheated her food and, bypassing the breakfast bar, made herself comfortable on the sofa and clicked on the television. Although she had a lot to think about, she'd maxed out all of her mental and emotional energy. Right now she would feed herself and the baby while watching mindless television.

But as she ate, Joni couldn't help but think about the changes that were about to come her way. She didn't know which would be good and which not so good, but she knew there would be a ripple effect. And she knew her relationship with Lex would change once more. Like it or not, he was going to be a big part of her life again.

Chapter Four

Joni looked at her reflection in the mirror and then sighed. There were no two ways about it. She looked terrible. The morning sickness had struck fast and furious this morning. She'd felt so nauseous and dizzy when she'd awakened that she'd wanted to stay in bed. But her stomach had begun to churn, and she'd managed to propel herself into the bathroom with barely a second to spare. Morning sickness was no joke.

After she'd emptied her stomach, she'd leaned against the wall until she was strong enough to stand. She couldn't be the only woman who suffered from severe morning sickness, so there must be a way to survive. Over the years Joni had become good friends with quite a few of the mothers she'd met through her job at the youth center. Under other circumstances she would ask any of them how they'd endured it.

But given the fact that she wasn't ready to reveal her pregnancy to anyone, she'd have to do without their remedies.

She took a quick shower, ate a piece of dry toast, which she was miraculously able to keep down, and got dressed in a pair of khaki shorts and a red top. Joni had hoped the bright color would disguise the weird tint of her skin, but it didn't. Although she didn't look like death warmed over, she still resembled the *Before* person in any number of makeup ads.

There was no avoiding it. She was going to have to put on makeup if she wanted to go out in public and not scare everyone she encountered. Otherwise her appearance would draw not only questions but concern as well. Since she didn't want to address inquiries about her health from everyone she met, she'd have to make sure she didn't look as bad as she felt.

After putting on blush and lipstick, Joni pronounced herself suitable to face the world. She shoved the makeup into her purse in case she needed to use it later in the day, then walked as fast as she dared down the stairs and to her car. Not surprisingly, laughter floated from her brother's open kitchen window. Brandon and Arden were the perfect couple, and no doubt they were goofing around as they cooked breakfast together.

Joni was happy Arden had come along when she had. Brandon had suffered a bad breakup years ago and had sworn off romantic relationships, throwing all of his emotions into building his restaurant. Then Arden's car broke down on the highway outside of Sweet Briar, and he'd stopped to help her. Before long the two of them had fallen in love and gotten married in a beautiful ceremony. Joni didn't begrudge them their happiness, but she wouldn't mind having a bit for herself.

She drove the short distance to the youth center and went to the gym. Every morning all of the children and volunteers gathered together for announcements. She told them of the day's plans as well as any upcoming events and acknowledged birthdays if there were any. Once that was done, the children scattered as they went to their various activities. Ordinarily Joni joined in a couple of activities, but today her stomach was still unsettled, so she went straight to her office instead.

Joni nibbled on saltines while filling out paperwork for grants. When lunchtime arrived, she felt better than she had when she'd awakened, although she was still a little nauseous. Her pulse sped up at the thought of seeing Lex again, and she frowned. She wasn't supposed to be interested in him that way. Even so, she freshened her makeup and ran a comb through her hair before she drove to the diner.

As luck would have it there was a parking spot available right in front. She snagged it and went inside. Even though it was not quite eleven thirty, the lunch crowd had descended, and Mabel's was doing brisk business. Most of the red vinyl booths and tables were filled, and the diner hummed with energy. Waitresses and waiters carrying trays filled with delicious-looking food walked expertly around the tables and chairs. People picking up to-go orders were clustered near the cash register by the front door. Joni spoke to those she knew and nodded to those she didn't as she made her way to the hostess, Tiffany.

"I'm meeting the mayor. Is he here?"

Tiffany nodded. "Yes. He's sitting at a booth in the back."

Joni glanced over Tiffany's shoulder. "I see him. I'll just go on over."

"Okay. Enjoy your lunch, Joni."

Joni wove around tables, exchanging greetings with friends as she made her way to the back booth. Lex generally sat near the front, making it easy for people who wanted to talk to reach him. Given the fact that she and Lex would be having a private conversation, she was relieved he'd taken a booth off the beaten path.

Lex was blessedly alone in his booth. He spotted her and immediately jumped to his feet as his good manners dictated. Being the recipient of his chivalrous behavior had spoiled her. Men who weren't as polite as Lex on a first date didn't get a second.

"How do you feel?" he asked after they sat down. His quiet voice reached her but wouldn't travel past the back of their booth.

She considered downplaying how ill she'd been that morning but decided against it. Although she would no longer share her innermost feelings with him, he had a vested interest in her health, at least as far as the baby went. Not only that, he'd seen her at her worst, so there was no sense in keeping things from him. Despite knowing they couldn't be overheard over the din in the restaurant, she leaned in closer to him and spoke softly. He leaned in as well.

"I was sick again this morning. I kind of expected it."

"Are you feeling better now?"

"A bit. I've been eating crackers all morning."

He nodded and gestured for their waiter. Brad, one

of the teens who frequented the youth center in the evenings, was beside their table in a blink of an eye.

"How can I help you?"

"Joni would like a mug of warm decaffeinated tea," Lex said, then looked at her. "It'll settle your stomach in no time."

"Okay. Would you like to order your lunch now?"

"We'll do that when you get back with the tea," Lex said.

The minute their server walked away, Joni kicked Lex as hard as she could.

He jumped. "Why did you do that?"

"Are you kidding? Why did you say what you did?" she whispered furiously. "Are you trying to broadcast to the entire town that I'm pregnant?"

"By ordering you a tea?"

He could not be that dense. "By saying in front of him that it would settle my stomach."

Lex shook his head. He took a deep breath and then spoke very gently. Soothingly. "I don't think saying something will settle your stomach is code for being pregnant. Especially to a teenage boy. Not only that, the kid just turned sixteen four days ago. This is his first day working at his first job. I know that because he told me. Twice. Trust me when I tell you that Brad is so excited to be working that nothing we say outside of our order will penetrate his mind. So relax and enjoy your food, okay?"

Chastised, Joni nodded. She was just being paranoid. Nobody could tell she was pregnant just by what she drank. "Okay. Sorry for kicking you."

Lex laughed. "No, you're not."

She laughed with him. "Okay. Then, I'm sorry for not being sorry."

"Apology, such as it is, accepted."

Brad returned with her tea and nearly spilled it on her as he set it on the table. "Sorry, Ms. Joni. This is my first day."

Joni smiled at the teenager. Despite the fact that he'd nearly scalded her, there was a broad smile on his face. She didn't doubt the sincerity of his apology. He was just too happy to keep from grinning. "No worries."

"Are you ready to order?"

"Yes."

"I can tell you about the specials," Brad said before launching into a long, memorized spiel. Even though Joni and Lex probably knew the specials better than he did, neither of them tried to stop him. When he was done, he grinned again. For a moment, Joni pictured her child as a teenager, and her heart stuttered. No, she was not going to allow herself to think that far ahead. She still had a pregnancy to get through.

After they placed their orders, Joni watched as Brad practically skipped to the kitchen. Yep, her secret was definitely safe. For now. She looked at Lex, who was stirring sugar into his coffee. "I don't want to tell anyone for a while."

"Not even Brandon or your parents?"

"Especially not them."

He covered her hand with his. His touch was at once soothing and disturbing. "They love you, Joni."

"I know. I'm just not ready to deal with all that now. I'm still trying to deal with it myself."

"Okay. I won't tell my family yet, either."

Joni paused, her teacup in the air. Why hadn't it occurred to her that Lex would tell his family about the baby? She'd met his parents and brothers several times, and she'd liked them. They were warm and openhearted people, and she knew they'd welcome her child with hugs and kisses.

Neither of them spoke for a minute, and as the silence stretched, Joni squirmed in her seat. She knew they needed to discuss the baby, but she didn't have the desire to bring up the topic. She thought Lex might push her to talk, but he didn't. Instead he took a sip of his coffee.

A few minutes later Brad returned with their lunch: soup and a sandwich for her, the Friday lunch special for Lex. Joni looked at Lex's meatloaf and mashed potatoes with envy. If she asked for a taste, she knew he would share. Her stomach rebelled at the thought. Bland was the way of meals for the foreseeable future.

Lex took a bite of his food and then began telling Joni about a book he'd just finished reading. She'd read it a few months ago and had suggested he might enjoy it. Apparently he had. They spent the rest of lunch having a spirited discussion about the feasibility of the murder plot. Talk about the book flowed into discussion about last night's basketball games. Although the adults had lost all three games, he was confident that, with the teens on their side, the men would win the upcoming battle of the sexes tournament. He grinned at her. "That is unless you cheat again."

Joni smirked. "We didn't cheat the other time. Every one of our players was either a teenager or a volunteer."

Two years ago the women's team had included the

Central Carolina University women's basketball team who'd been reigning NCAA Division II champions. They'd creamed the men, and the women had enjoyed bragging rights for the year.

"Well, no matter how many ringers you have this year, we'll win. Our high-school kids are fantastic."

"And the adults?" Joni asked.

"Let's just say I'll try to steer some of them in other directions where their actual talents might lie. Like leading the cheers."

Joni laughed. As she set her spoon into her empty bowl she realized that she and Lex hadn't resolved anything. It had been so easy to fall into their old rapport and talk about any and everything. But she couldn't hide from reality by pretending nothing had changed. "We haven't decided anything."

"What were we supposed to decide?"

The question flummoxed her. They hadn't set a topic for today's lunch. She hadn't thought they needed to. "How we're going to handle things between us."

"What do you suggest?"

"I need some distance, Lex. I need time and space to deal with everything."

"I don't agree. The way I see it, we're in this thing together. So we may as well get used to being together. To be honest, I'm not having a problem being with you."

"How nice for you." She hadn't meant to sound bitter, but she knew that was the way it came out. Why couldn't she just get over her anger? Life would be simpler if she could.

"I don't want to upset you. Why don't we save this conversation for another time?"

"Because putting it off won't change anything. I really need some time on my own to try and figure out things."

"How much time?"

"I don't know."

He blew out a breath, and she prepared herself for an argument. "Fine. But you need to remember one thing."

"What's that?"

"You're not on your own. Of course you can make decisions by yourself if they only affect you. But I plan on being involved in matters that affect the baby."

She had to give him credit for being reasonable. "That's fair."

Brad returned with their bill, putting a halt to the rest of their conversation. Fortunately the teen didn't linger. Lex picked up the check before she could. She reached for it, and he waved her hand away. "I'll take care of it, Joni."

"I thought we agreed that I would pick up the next check."

"I invited you, so today doesn't count."

"Lex."

"It's only lunch. And considering the fact that my child is currently growing inside you, it's the least I can do. I can't provide nourishment the way you can."

His voice was filled with something that sounded like admiration, and her heart warmed. "Well, when you put it that way… Fine. I accept."

"Glad to hear it." Lex beckoned for Brad to come and collect their payment. "Keep the change."

Brad looked from the check to the cash and grinned. "Thanks a lot, Mayor."

"You're welcome."

Joni and Lex walked through the diner without stopping to talk to anyone. When they reached her car, he looked at her, a sheepish grin on his face. "You're going to have to see a doctor soon."

"I know. But that's not something I want to discuss in the middle of Main Street."

"Agreed. I'll stop by later today so we can talk." He held the door open for her, and she slid into the driver's seat. She swallowed her protest. After all, she was the one who'd said she didn't want to talk in the middle of the street. Pulling into traffic, she tried not to think about seeing Lex again. Although she'd asked for distance, she had a feeling it was going to be harder to achieve than she'd believed.

Lex watched as Joni drove away, then sighed with relief. That had gone better than he'd anticipated. They'd actually shared an enjoyable, stress-free meal. Given how strained their few interactions had been this past month and a half, he hadn't known what to expect. When Joni had sat down across from him, her tension had been obvious in the stiffness of her shoulders and the way she'd held her oversize purse in front of her body like a shield. The residual effects of their night together hadn't diminished. She was still angry with him. Truthfully he was angry and disappointed with himself. He'd never lost control like that before.

Despite how badly he'd screwed up everything, Lex had hoped that Joni's attitude toward him would soften over time and that she would forgive him. True they'd just had a pleasant lunch, but the tension was still there, as was her anger.

He'd begun to fear they'd never get their friendship back. Not that he'd ever give up on having Joni in his life. She meant too much to him to just let her vanish without a fight. Now there was their child to fight for as well. His heart thudded in his chest. He was going to be a father again. This time he would do a better job of protecting his baby.

Realizing he'd been frozen in place, he turned and began walking to city hall. There weren't many people about, so he made it to his office in a few minutes. After speaking to Mrs. Harper, Lex went to his office. There were a couple of things he needed to take care of before the end of the day, and it took all of his will-power to stay on task. The people of Sweet Briar were counting on him to do his job to the best of his ability, so he couldn't slack off just because his life had taken an unexpected turn.

When he'd finalized the budget and had confirmed his meeting with the owners of the Willow Creek bowling alley, Lex shut down his computer and headed out of the office.

If Joni was this concerned about keeping her pregnancy a secret, he doubted she would do anything that might even remotely draw attention to herself. He'd respect her need for privacy, but not at the expense of their baby. Although he thought she was being paranoid, he didn't want to give her another reason to put a higher wall between them or increase the distance between them. Willow Creek should be far enough away. And since he had a meeting there that afternoon, he would kill two birds with one stone.

Sweet Briar was situated on the ocean and had a stretch of some of the most beautiful beaches in all of North Carolina. Under Lex's guidance, the once-dying town was experiencing a renaissance. Previously struggling businesses were now thriving, and new businesses had opened. People had begun to move to the city instead of away. Summer tourists were visiting in record numbers.

Lex loved being the mayor. He enjoyed interacting with the citizens and doing his best to improve their lives. But today, he was glad to have a reason to leave town for a while. The solitary, forty-five minute ride would hopefully be enough time for him to get his head on straight.

The day was warm with a slight breeze, so Lex lowered his windows to let the fresh air blow into the car. As he traveled down the highway, he kept picturing Joni as she'd looked during lunch. When she'd arrived, she'd looked so sick he'd half expected her to bolt from the table and into the ladies' room. Fortunately she'd looked much better after she'd eaten. He hoped that would last.

Caroline had been the picture of health when she'd been pregnant. He couldn't recall even one day when she'd suffered from morning sickness. Everything had gone perfectly with her pregnancy, yet the unthinkable had happened. Joni wasn't doing nearly as well as Caroline had. Did that mean he'd lose this child, too? His insides shook at the very idea. There was no way he could survive that kind of loss again. His heart would break into a million pieces, but this time he wouldn't be able to put it together again.

Honestly, he wasn't sure he'd managed to put all of the pieces of his heart back together the first time. When Caroline had walked out on him, she'd taken his ability to love with her. His relationship with Joni had been his longest-lasting one with a woman since his marriage ended, and they were only friends. Given his unwillingness to risk his heart again, the possibility of another child hadn't existed.

Could he open himself up to loving a child again? As hurt as he'd been by the divorce, it was the loss of Briana that had brought him to his knees. Seeing his once active baby lying lifeless had been like having his heart ripped from his chest and thrown onto the floor. If he could have, he would have traded places with her. He'd even prayed to. Yet at the end of the day, his daughter had been the one lowered into the dark grave, while he'd been forced to live without her.

Over time he'd learned to be happy again, although the hole in his heart had never closed. He didn't expect it to. But he'd found satisfaction by being able to contribute to society. He'd been able to make new friends. He knew he would be able to support his child and Joni financially. But open his heart to this baby the way he'd opened it to Briana? He wasn't sure he was up to the risk. Maybe he should let Joni push him out of her life now the way she wanted to, but he couldn't. He hadn't been raised to walk away from family. A father provided for his child. Somehow he was going to have to do what was right. He'd just have to manage to do that and protect his heart at the same time.

He reached the highway exit for Willow Creek and pulled onto the ramp. The ride hadn't provided him with the tranquility he'd been hoping for, but he couldn't allow himself to wallow in self-pity. There was business to be handled for Sweet Briar, so he needed to stop thinking about himself.

After checking his watch, he decided he had enough time for a quick stop before his meeting, so he dashed into the big-box store and purchased a few items. He stashed the bag in the trunk of his car, then went to his meeting with Randy and Melanie Gilmore, a brother and sister team who owned the Willow Creek bowling alley. They were impressed with his presentation on Sweet Briar and the feasibility of opening a second bowling alley there. They promised to get back to him after they ran his financials past their accountant.

The meeting concluded, Lex shook their hands, then walked back to his car. Willow Creek was a nice midsize town and had many amenities that Sweet Briar lacked at the moment, but in Lex's estimation it couldn't compare to his town in the charm department.

Lex's mood was greatly improved on his ride back to Sweet Briar. Rather than head straight home, he headed for the youth center. It was around dinnertime, so the little kids would be gone, leaving only the teenagers who liked to play basketball or video games. Joni usually stuck around for another hour or so, just to make sure there were no problems before she left. He'd thought about waiting until she was at home to give her the items he'd picked up for her but decided against it. Stopping by at work seemed less intrusive than visiting her at home. Since she wanted distance between them, this was the better of the two options.

Lex pulled into the parking lot, then grabbed the bag from the trunk of his car. Paul Stephens was coming out the front door, his nephew and two young nieces by his side. Lex waved to the small family as they got into the car. It was common knowledge that Roz Martin, Paul's sister-in-law, was battling cancer.

Joni and Charlotte had organized a group of women to help the family as much as possible. They'd created a schedule for people to drop off dinner at least three times a week. Others assisted with household chores.

When Lex stepped inside the center, he took a minute to look around. Although people were moving quickly as they left, everyone was smiling. Joni did a great job of thinking of fun activities that kept the kids begging to come here every day. She worked long hours for little pay. If she continued to suffer from morning sickness, she was going to have no choice but to cut back on her hours. He hoped she would stop being ill for several reasons, chief among them the way seeing her ill tore at his heart, but that wasn't something he could control.

Lex strode to Joni's office. The door was open, and her back was to him. She was rummaging through a file drawer. Sometime during the day, she'd pulled her hair into a ponytail, making her look even younger than she was. He allowed himself a moment to soak in her beauty before he knocked on her door. She looked over her shoulder at him and froze briefly before she smiled. He knew her well enough to recognize the cool smile she reserved for corporate or political events. It wasn't the smile that she used to give him. Pushing aside his disappointment and pain, he stepped into the office and closed the door behind him.

"I picked up a couple of things for you."

Her smile turned quizzical. "What things?"

He held up the bag but didn't hand it over to her. Over the years he'd learned how much Joni loved gifts. They didn't have to be expensive. Heck, she'd exclaimed just as happily over a chocolate bar as she did over the designer perfume he'd had made especially for her. Perfume that smelled so good on her it nearly drove him out of his mind with every breath he took. Perfume that had been particularly potent one night.

"It's nothing big. Just some things I think you'll need." He offered her the bag.

"You know, it's the thought that counts." This time her smile was sweet and sincere. Warm.

She reached inside the bag and pulled out a bottle. She looked at the label and then back at him. "Prenatal vitamins?"

"Yes."

"Where did you get these? And when?" Her tone was frantic.

"I picked them up today." He held up a hand to forestall any complaint she might have. "I had to go to Willow Creek for a meeting. I had a few minutes, so I got them for you. I know you haven't had a chance to visit a doctor, but I believe you need these."

Calm again, she smiled at his words. "I planned on going to Walmart out on the highway and picking some up when I got off work. Now I don't have to do that. Thank you."

Relief surged through him. He hadn't been certain how she would react. In fact, she might have accused him of overreaching. "There's more."

"I know." Joni reached inside the bag again and pulled out a book. "*What to Expect When You're Expecting.*"

"I know that you've never been pregnant before, and I thought you'd have questions. From what I've been told, this is one of the best books for women looking for information about their pregnancy."

She pulled the book to her chest and closed her eyes. When she spoke, her voice was soft. A tear slid down her face. "Thank you so much. I can't tell you how much I appreciate this."

Lex quickly closed the distance between them and put his arm around her shoulders. "Oh, Joni, you know I would do anything for you. All you have to do is ask."

She leaned her head against his shoulder and sniffed. Although Joni was a person who wasn't afraid to share her emotions, she didn't often cry. Lex was at a loss for what to do besides pat her back and tell her that she would be fine. Of course, he knew her hormones were at least partly responsible for her emotional response. Knowing that didn't help, though. He hated to see Joni cry no matter the reason. Fortunately only a few more tears fell.

Joni lifted her head and smiled. "Sorry about that."

He brushed the pad of his thumb across her cheek, wiping away the wetness. "You don't need to apologize."

She stepped out of his arms, and he missed her nearness. "Thanks. I appreciate these gifts."

He could tell she was about to usher him out of her office. "There is one more thing."

She held the bag upside down. "Not in here."

"It's something I want to discuss with you. You haven't mentioned going to the doctor. That's important, and you should do it sooner rather than later."

"I know. I've already scheduled an appointment with the obstetrician who delivered Carmen's twins."

"When's the appointment?"

"Next Friday. Why?"

"Because I want to come with you."

Chapter Five

"You want to come with me?" Joni knew she'd heard Lex correctly, yet shocked, she could only parrot what he'd said.

"Of course. Why do you sound so surprised?"

And why did he sound so disappointed? Didn't he understand how hurt and confused she was by the entire situation? Didn't he have any clue about the conflicting emotions that continually bombarded her? She felt joy, misery, anger and everything in between. Sometimes all at once. She had yet to get her feelings under control. She'd never regain her equilibrium with him around.

That's why she needed to stay away from him. She didn't want him around when she was filled with negative emotions. She might say or do something to hurt him again. Guilt consumed her every time she thought of what she'd told him last night. She'd actually said she didn't like him. Truth be told, she'd come close to saying that she hated him. There was no telling how badly he would have been hurt had she actually uttered those words. Not that she'd lied. But still, if she couldn't say anything nice, she should at least be quiet. Until she was able to get herself under control, she needed to keep her distance from him for his sake as well as her own.

"I guess I'm surprised because I told you I needed space. Going with me to the doctor is the exact opposite of that."

He exhaled slowly. "Joni, I'm not trying to crowd you. I just want to be a part of my child's life."

"I have no intention of keeping you out of *our* child's life. But the baby won't be born for several months."

"I know that, but…"

"But what?"

"I'd like to be a part of everything from the beginning. Including the pregnancy."

"I get that. And when I'm further along and having an ultrasound where you can actually see the baby, you can come with me. But that's not going to happen this time. There won't be anything for you to see. I don't mean to sound harsh, but your presence isn't necessary."

Lex nodded. Joni knew she'd hurt him, but she needed to think of herself and what she needed. And what she needed right now was peace of mind so she could deliver a healthy baby. She'd never be at ease with Lex lurking around every corner of her life.

"Okay. But since you haven't told anyone about

your pregnancy, I need you to promise you'll call me if you need anything, no matter how small."

"Lex."

"I'll worry about you. And the baby."

She sighed. He wasn't making it easy to keep him at a distance. She couldn't accuse him of using the baby in order to get close to her. He truly cared about the baby. "Okay. I promise I'll call if I need anything."

"And I promise to drop everything and come." His quietly spoken words were a vow she could count on. He shoved his hands into his pants pockets. "And on that note, I'll get out of here. Have a good evening."

"Thanks again for everything."

"You're very welcome." Lex took one step toward the door, then paused as if debating. A second later, he leaned down and brushed his lips against hers in a gentle kiss. Then, without another word, he left.

Stunned, Joni put a hand to her mouth. He'd kissed her. Her heart started to soar, but she clipped its wings. She couldn't allow herself to get swept away by a simple goodbye kiss. Just as she couldn't allow Lex to accompany her to the doctor. She needed to stay strong. It would be so easy to lean on him. She knew that eventually he would be around because of the baby, but not yet. She needed time and space now to get back on an even keel and learn to stand on her own two feet.

She had to admit that Lex's thoughtful gifts had softened her heart a bit. Not enough to make her change her mind about her need for space, but enough to make her smile at his sweetness.

Joni tucked the book and vitamins into her purse, then got back to work. It took about an hour to finalize the schedule and order the supplies for the upcoming quarter. Once that was finished, she straightened her desk and shut down her computer, grabbed her purse, locked her office and hopped into her car to drive home. Out of nowhere she was suddenly ravenous, so she decided to go by Brandon's restaurant. She'd never believed cravings were a real thing, but suddenly she desperately wanted seafood crepes. But since that was one of her favorite meals, she didn't make a big deal of it. She was eager to get home and open her new book and discover whether cravings were a medical phenomenon and, if so, what they meant.

It occurred to her that she was going to have to start cooking on a regular basis. Although Brandon would happily cook meals for her child as he did for her, she knew that wouldn't be right. The baby wasn't his responsibility. It was hers. And though Lex was a good cook, she would still need to cook when the child was with her.

It wasn't as if the cooking gene had skipped her. She knew what to do. She just didn't find pleasure in making the same meals over and over for weeks and years on end. The monotony would be soul-crushing. But people had done it for generations and lived to tell the tale. And who knew, maybe she could find new recipes and vary the meals she made.

Joni pulled into the employee parking lot and then went inside the restaurant. As expected, the place was packed. World-renowned food critics had rated Heaven on Earth as one of the best restaurants in the region a couple of years ago. Ever since then, there had been a long wait for reservations. But Brandon always held a couple of tables open for the citizens of Sweet Briar who'd supported him when he was just starting out. And of course as his sister, she never had to wait.

"Hey, Joni. Are you here to help out?" Margo, the hostess, asked. "We're two people short."

Joni groaned. Brandon was a sweetheart, but he was also a perfectionist. Though he paid a generous salary and provided full benefits to all of his employees, he had the hardest time keeping a full complement of waitstaff. To be fair, it wasn't all his fault. Some people couldn't live up to his standards and soon quit after realizing what would be required of them. Others worked for Brandon long enough to save money for college. Whatever the cause, it seemed like Brandon was always in need of servers. Since her brother had done so much to support her, she kept a waitress uniform in his office and helped him whenever she could.

"What happened?"

"Stacy's husband was in a car accident this afternoon. And who knows what happened to Rebecca. She just didn't show. That's twice in two weeks. This time she didn't even bother to call. I don't know why Brandon keeps her around."

Joni thought she knew. Rebecca was a recent war widow. She'd moved to Sweet Briar with her children to stay with her elderly aunt and get a fresh start. Brandon and Joni's brother was career military, and they did what they could to support military families. Joni made a mental note to contact Rebecca to see if the other woman and her family needed anything. Although that wasn't necessarily in her job description as director of the youth center, a part of her would always be a social worker. She could never turn her back on anyone in need. Which was why she was going to put on her waitress uniform and work for a couple of hours instead of going home like she'd planned.

"I'll let Brandon know I'm here. What tables do you want me to cover?"

Once Joni had her assignment, she went into the kitchen. She stood back a second and watched as her brother plated meals and then handed them to a waiting server. He looked up at her. "Here to help?"

"Just until the rush ends."

"Thanks."

Joni snagged two warm rolls, then went into her brother's office to change. As she slipped on her uniform, Joni ate the delicious bread. Her hunger wasn't anywhere near sated, but she no longer felt like she would keel over if she didn't get something into her stomach.

Once she was dressed, Joni grabbed a pad and pen and went into the main dining room. As luck would have it, Lex was at one of her tables, perusing a menu. A man and a woman she didn't recognize were seated across from him, studying their menus as well. The trio looked up when Joni approached. The couple smiled, but Lex looked annoyed. Joni couldn't fathom why.

Deciding to ignore Lex, she turned to the couple. "My name is Joni, and I'll be your server tonight. Would you like to order drinks and appetizers, or would you like a little more time to study the menu?"

The woman opened her mouth, but before she could utter a word, Lex spoke. "Just what do you think you're doing?"

"I'm trying to take your order. Why, what does it look like I'm doing?"

Instead of answering, Lex pushed to his feet and took Joni by the elbow. "Excuse us for a minute."

Joni didn't want to cause a scene, so she didn't protest as Lex steered her through the dining room and out the front door. However, her temper was rising, and by the time they'd stepped outside, her anger was close to boiling over. She snatched her arm from his hand, spun around and glared at him. "Just what do you think *you're* doing?"

"I just asked you the same thing."

"I'm helping my brother. The same as I've done numerous times over the years, as you well know."

"That was then. You're in no condition to do that now."

"I'm fine."

"You've been sick more than once this week that I know of, including this morning. So don't tell me you're fine."

A well-dressed older couple was approaching the entrance of the restaurant, so Joni grabbed Lex's hand and pulled him down the street. Despite the anger and frustration currently simmering below the surface, Joni's skin tingled at the contact. This was so not good. She and Lex weren't going to have a physical relationship in the future, so she needed to stop reacting like this. They weren't lovers. They were barely friends.

When they reached the corner, Joni looked around. The streetlamps illuminating the sidewalks revealed that they were alone. Good. She didn't need witnesses to this conversation. "You know good and well why I was nauseous, so don't act as if I have some fatal disease."

"That's not what I'm doing. But you know you need

to be careful." He lowered his voice to a furious whisper. "It's important for you to take care of yourself, especially in the first trimester. You don't want to lose the baby."

"I'm waiting tables for a couple of hours. It's not as if I'm out here chopping down trees. I'm just walking back and forth."

"Carrying heavy trays."

"Something I've done many times before."

"You just got off work."

"Where I spent most of my time sitting and playing with kids. Neither of those things is strenuous."

"That's not the point. You need to eat right and take care of yourself." He frowned. "Have you eaten dinner yet?"

"I grabbed something."

His eyes narrowed at her vague reply. "You were coming here to get something to eat, weren't you? Then they asked you to work. Don't deny it. I've seen it happen enough times to know that's what happened. You should have said no."

There was not going to be any getting through to him. And as he just pointed out, she'd been asked to help out on more than one occasion. He'd seen her do it and knew that she was capable. "I've got to go. And you have to get back to your guests."

She took a step away from him.

"This isn't over, Joni."

His voice wasn't loud or threatening, but the determination she heard made her shiver. Still, she couldn't let him have the last word. "It is for me."

"It is for *now*. We'll revisit this later."

As she walked back to the restaurant, Joni was annoyed that he was beside her. Of course, since they were going to the same place, it only made sense. When they reached the door, he held it open for her. She swept inside and then went to his table to take orders.

He sat down and smiled at his guests. "Sorry about that. We had something to clear up."

"No problem." The couple exchanged glances. "We needed time to make up our minds on what we want. Everything looks so good, it was hard to decide."

"You can't go wrong with anything."

Joni took their orders and promised to be right back with their beverages. Picking up their menus, she returned to the kitchen. Somehow she had to make it through the next couple of hours. Of course, with Lex watching her every move, it wasn't going to be easy.

Lex stared as Joni stalked into the kitchen. She seemed okay, but he knew that outward appearances could mask a host of problems. There was no way he would be able to make her see reason tonight. She was too furious for that. Perhaps later when she cooled down, she would realize that she needed to take better care of herself and that waitressing was a bad idea.

"So that's Joni."

Lex met the amused stares of his favorite cousin, Sophia, and her husband, Andrew, who Lex considered a good friend. "How did you know?"

"She introduced herself when she came to the table. I thought Aunt Regina said she worked at the youth center."

"She does. Her brother owns this restaurant, and for a reason that escapes me, he's unable to hold on to good employees. Joni helps out from time to time." Lex took a swallow of his water, trying to flush his irritation. "And just what did my mother tell you about Joni?"

Sophia pretended to lock her lips. "You know I'll never tell. What we discuss is strictly confidential."

"But you have no problem letting me know you were discussing Joni."

"None at all."

Lex snorted. His parents had six sons and no daughters, so his mother was very close to her nieces, especially Sophia, who was most like her. Both of them were mischievous with wicked senses of humor. Neither of them took themselves too seriously. He didn't press Sophia for an answer. He knew she'd never tell. But then, she'd held a few of his confidences over the years, so he hadn't expected her to. Since he knew both her and his mother, he was confident nothing they'd said had been vicious. Neither of them had a mean bone in her body. Besides, he knew his mother adored Joni.

Joni returned with their drinks and appetizers. She distributed them, and then she was gone. His eyes followed her as she went to another table where three men were eating. One of them said something, and Joni laughed. The sound awakened the desire Lex had tried so hard to suppress. That emotion was quickly followed up by unreasonable jealousy. A stranger had made Joni laugh, while lately all he did was make her frown.

"So what brings you to Sweet Briar?" Lex asked, forcing his eyes away from Joni's backside. Funny how he'd never noticed how perfect it looked in her black uniform skirt. Her waist was still tiny, but he could imagine how she would look in a few months as their baby grew inside her.

"My job," Andrew said. "I had a settlement conference in Charlotte, so Sophia decided to come along with me to make a long weekend of it."

"Are you staying in Sweet Briar?"

"No. We're going to visit my parents in Hilton Head." Andrew bit into an appetizer. "This is probably the best thing I've ever eaten in my life. Sophia, why don't you ever make me food like this?"

Sophia laughed. She was a fabulous pastry chef and sold her desserts to restaurants in the New York area. "I guess I could learn. Of course, that means no more macarons for a while."

"Never mind. We'll just have to convince the chef to open a restaurant in New York."

"No chance of that," Lex interjected. "Brandon is a fixture in town."

"In that case, we'll have to fly down regularly."

"Okay. I'll pretend that you'll be dropping by to visit me and not for the food."

Andrew laughed.

"Seriously," Lex said, "I'm glad you stopped by. I have lots of friends in town, but I still miss my family."

"You know, planes fly both ways. You could always come visit us," Sophia said.

"I plan to. I just get so busy. There's so much that needs doing. Running a town is a lot of work."

"Just don't become a workaholic again. Take time to focus on the things and people in your life that matter." Sophia squeezed his hand as she emphasized her point. "The town will always be here. But people won't wait around forever."

"I know." He'd had the same conversation with his parents on several occasions. It wasn't as if he planned to neglect his family. It was just that he got busy, and time got away from him. The citizens of Sweet Briar were counting on him to give his best. He'd never given less than his all when he'd worked for his family business, and he had no intention of giving less now. Still, he knew he had to find time for the people who mattered most.

Joni returned carrying a tray containing their meals. It took all of his self-control to not jump up and snatch the tray away from her. That would only upset and embarrass her. Not only that, he would probably cause her to drop their food, which would really tick her off. With his cousin watching their every move, he didn't want to draw any more attention. His family knew that he and Joni were friends. She'd actually accompanied him to New York a couple of times. But what they didn't know was that she was pregnant with his child. Since she wanted to keep that a secret for the time being, he needed to behave in a manner that didn't raise additional suspicions.

After setting their meals in front of them, Joni put the empty appetizer dishes on the tray. "Is there anything else I can get for you?"

"No, thanks," Sophia said.

"Enjoy your dinner."

Without even tasting it, Lex knew his meal was cooked to perfection. Still, there was no way he was going to be able to enjoy it with Joni working when she should be at home resting. He knew he'd agreed to give her space, but if she refused to listen to reason, then all bets were off.

Chapter Six

Joni lay back in the tub, letting the warm water soothe her aching back. She hadn't intended to work more than an hour at the restaurant, but after Lex had all but ordered her to leave, she'd stayed three more hours. It wasn't as if she was fragile. Many women waited tables well into their final trimester. Not that she intended to be one of them. But she was strong. And stubborn, she admitted to herself with a rueful laugh.

Lex had frowned at her whenever she'd come to his table, and he'd stared at her when she'd been serving others. Thankfully he'd been gone by the time she'd left, carrying two plates piled high with food. She'd eaten the seafood crepes for dinner and saved the blackened salmon, rice pilaf and steamed broccoli for lunch tomorrow. Saturdays were slower at the youth center, since a lot of families chose to spend the weekend together, but Joni liked to pop in for a few hours in the morning and touch base with the teens who came to play basketball or make jewelry.

Joni let her mind wander, but when the water got cold enough to raise goose bumps on her skin, she got out of the tub and toweled off. Before she put on pajamas, she studied her body in her full-size mirror. She turned from side to side, but there were no visible changes in her body. Not that she expected to see anything yet. She quickly dressed and hopped into bed. She'd planned on reading a little of the book Lex had given her, but that was before she'd worked all night. Now all she wanted to do was sleep.

She stretched her arms over the cool sheet. The bed suddenly felt empty, which didn't make a lick of sense. She'd slept alone in this bed for years. Yet now she longed for someone to be there beside her, cradling her in his strong arms as she drifted off to sleep. And not a nameless, faceless someone. She yearned for Lex. Perhaps she was thinking about him because he was the father of her baby. Naturally she'd want the man who'd fathered her child sleeping by her side while she was pregnant. But she needed to stop thinking that way. Thanks to the baby they'd created, Lex would always be a part of her life. But he'd be a partner in raising their child and not a romantic partner. He'd been clear about that. The sooner she got that through her head, the better off she'd be.

Joni turned on her side and closed her eyes. Hopefully sleep would come easily.

She slept well for several hours, but around five in the morning she awakened, nauseous. Flinging herself out of bed, she dashed into the bathroom, barely making it to the toilet in time. Once she'd emptied her stomach, she rinsed her mouth and staggered into the kitchen. She filled a mug with water and microwaved it for tea, then returned to her room and plopped onto her bed.

She rubbed her stomach. Even though she couldn't feel the life growing inside her, she was filled with happiness just knowing that her body was nourishing a little person. "You're making Mommy sick there, bud. We're going to have to work on a way to peacefully coexist," she said softly.

Since she wasn't sleepy, Joni piled her pillows behind her back and grabbed the baby book from her nightstand. She skimmed the chapters until she found one on morning sickness. She'd been around enough pregnant women to know it was normal, but she needed to be sure that the frequency and ferocity of her sickness wasn't unusual. Joni had been sick more than in the mornings. Some days her sickness lasted well into the afternoon. She didn't want to wait until her appointment with her doctor to find out whether this was abnormal, if waiting would put her child at risk. After reading that being sick in the afternoon wasn't unusual, Joni was able to relax.

She sipped her tea and flipped through the book, reading bits of various chapters for another hour, then decided to get up. The tea had soothed her stomach, and now she was hungry. Most days, Joni wore shorts and cute tops to work. That way she was able to participate in any number of activities, from finger painting to baseball, without worrying about ruining her clothes. On Saturdays she preferred to dress up a bit, since the center would be quieter and she wouldn't be doing any of those things. She pulled on a floral cotton skirt that skimmed her knees, a coordinating knit top and low-heeled sandals. Deciding to leave her hair loose, she ran a comb through it, then brushed it behind her ears.

When she reached the bottom of the stairs, she ran into Brandon and Arden.

"What are you doing up so early?" Arden asked.

"I couldn't sleep. I'm going to the diner for breakfast, then to work. I have some paperwork that needs doing. I don't need to ask where the two of you are headed."

"We need to get to the fish and produce markets early if we want to get the freshest ingredients. Unfortunately we were delayed a bit this morning," Brandon said. He looked at Arden, who flushed as she got into the car. After closing Arden's door, Brandon walked over to Joni. "If you wait a while, you can join us for breakfast."

"Thanks, but no. As Granddad used to say, my stomach is gnawing on my backbone."

Brandon laughed, then opened her car door. "I'll see you later."

Joni waited until her brother drove off, then followed him down the driveway and through the quiet streets. The day was overcast, which was no surprise, since the weather forecast called for rain later that afternoon. It looked like the weatherman was right.

Someone was pulling out of a space half a block from the diner, and Joni pulled right in. Two days in a row. The parking gods were being very good to her.

Joni stepped into Mabel's Diner and inhaled the appetizing aromas. She hesitated for a second to see if her stomach would rebel, but luckily it didn't. The last thing Joni wanted was to be spotted sprinting to the bathroom. That would definitely set tongues a-wagging. Not that any of the talk would be vicious. But it didn't have to be in order to be harmful. Joni didn't want to be the subject of speculation.

She waved to a group of older men who hung out in front of the barbershop most afternoons. Neither rain nor sleet nor dark of night could keep them from getting together.

Although there was a good crowd, Joni found an empty booth near the back. She was just setting her purse beside her when a shadow fell over her table. Her pulse sped up, and she knew immediately who it was.

"Mind if I join you?" Lex asked.

"And if I say yes?"

"I'll leave you to eat in peace." He gestured to the men she'd just waved to. All four of them were watching Joni and Lex. Mr. Harris even waved. "Of course, the town criers will wonder why we're eating at separate tables."

"You could always get your food to go," Joni grumbled.

"Nah." Lex winked, and her heart skipped a beat. "That would be criminal."

Joni nodded. She really didn't want to eat alone anyway. "Fine. Sit down. That way you can apologize to me."

"For what?" he asked as he sat down across from her. Their knees brushed, and a tingle raced down her spine. She ignored it. She needed to stay focused.

"Last night. You were incredibly rude."

He glanced down at his hands. When he looked up

again, his expression was sheepish. "You're right. I was out of line. I guess I overreacted."

"You guess?"

"Okay. I overreacted. I know you put in long hours at the youth center. Then you put in even more at the restaurant. You're only one person. You can't do it all. I don't want you to get run-down."

"That's fair." She blew out a breath. "I forgive you."

"Thanks."

Their waitress came over. After filling Lex's coffee cup, she took their orders. Joni was feeling a bit better and decided that her stomach could handle pancakes. At least, she hoped so.

They didn't talk much as Lex doctored his coffee. Joni loved coffee and knew the next months of not having even a drop would be torture. But she'd willingly make the sacrifice in order to protect the health of her child. She'd learn to make do with herbal tea or juice.

Joni took a swallow of her orange juice. "So how long are your cousin and her husband going to be in town?"

"They're already gone. They were passing through on their way to South Carolina."

Over the years, Joni had heard so much about his favorite cousin. "I'm glad I finally got to meet her. Too bad we didn't get the opportunity to talk."

"Don't worry. You'll get your chance. She and her husband plan to come back to town in a couple of months. We'll have dinner."

"I don't think that's such a good idea."

"Don't say no, Joni. I've been trying to get you and Sophia together for years. I want you to get to know my family better. Especially now."

Joni sighed. Although he hadn't mentioned the baby, she knew their child factored into his thinking. And he was right. It would be easier on all of them if she knew his family as well as he knew hers. Her parents visited Sweet Briar several times a year. Each time they came, she and Lex entertained them. Her parents absolutely adored Lex. He and Brandon were good friends. Only her brother Russell, who was stationed overseas, hadn't had the opportunity to spend much time with Lex. No doubt he would like him just as much as the rest of her family did. "Okay."

After that was agreed upon, Lex seemed to relax. Joni realized this situation couldn't be easy on him, either. After all, he hadn't planned on making a baby. But now that they had, he was doing his best to step up. He probably felt as though he was on the outside looking in. Joni vowed to be more considerate of his feelings, even though she knew she couldn't let him get too close. Pregnant women weren't always logical, and she needed to think with her brain. She couldn't let her emotions cloud her behavior. If she wasn't careful, she might do something ridiculous like ask him to spend the night so she could fall asleep in his arms.

Two people came up to Lex to ask questions, saving Joni the need to make conversation. It was hard to believe that only a few months ago they could talk for hours about anything. Other times they sat in peaceful silence. Today's conversation seemed to take more effort, and the silence was anything but restful. It was awkward. It was hard to believe how much damage they'd done to their relationship in one night. Making love brought most people closer together. It had pushed her and Lex so far apart they might as well be living in different countries. She couldn't see how they would ever be friends again.

The sorrow she felt at that thought must have shown on her face because, after the couple left, Lex turned back to her. He took one look at her and covered her hand with his. "What's wrong?"

She sighed. "Nothing."

"Come on, Joni. I know you too well for that. Talk to me."

"I wish I could. It used to be so easy between us. Now everything is a mess, and I don't have any idea how to fix it." To her horror, her voice trembled, and her eyes filled with tears.

"Don't cry."

"It's just these stupid hormones."

"Whatever the cause, it rips me apart to see you in tears."

He pressed a piece of fabric into her hands. Lex had to be the only man under sixty who still carried a handkerchief. She'd teased him about it in the past, and he'd laughed. Thinking about how much their friendship had changed made her cry even harder. She tried to make herself stop, but she couldn't.

Lex rose and walked to her side of the booth. "Scoot over."

She slid across the seat, and he sat beside her and wrapped his arm around her. Without thinking, she pressed her head against his chest. Inhaling, she got a whiff of his all too familiar scent. Being in his arms reminded her of how desperately she'd yearned for him last night. She'd wanted him to hold her, and now he was. Gradually her tears slowed and then stopped. She sniffled. "I'm sorry. I never expected to turn into one of those blubbering women who cry at the drop of a hat."

Lex laughed then spoke softly. "I thought you said it was the hormones. If you're right then you should return to your normal self in a few months."

Joni smiled and snuggled closer, allowing herself an extended moment of comfort. "I don't think that's the case. In a few months the baby will be a whole lot bigger. I probably won't recognize my body."

"You'll look different. But you'll be as beautiful as always."

Lex's words lifted Joni's heart, touching her in a way she hadn't been prepared for. She straightened and moved away. She couldn't let herself believe he felt anything romantic for her. He'd already shown her that he didn't. Lex was charming by nature, and compliments slipped easily from his lips. They were sincere, but she didn't want to misinterpret them. She wiped her face with the handkerchief and offered it to him.

"Keep it. In case your hormones get the best of you again."

"Thanks." She shoved it into her purse.

"What are you going to do today?"

"I've got work to do at the center. Speaking of which, I need to get going." She looked at Lex pointedly, and he slid out of the booth, standing aside to let her out. She dug through her purse and pulled out her wallet. Although he didn't say anything, she could sense Lex wanted to grab the check and pay it. This wasn't a new battle. He'd always tried to pay the bill whenever they'd gone out. In the years they'd known each other, she'd been victorious roughly thirty percent of the time. The imbalance hadn't bothered her then because they'd been friends. She'd understood that that was the way Lex demonstrated his affection. And she'd shown hers in other ways, so it had equaled out. But they weren't friends now.

"Take care of yourself," he said.

"I will."

Joni dropped enough cash on the table to cover the bill and a generous tip and walked through the diner. When she reached the front, she stared out the window. The rain was coming down in buckets. She thought of the umbrella she kept in her car. The weatherman had said rain later *this afternoon*. It was still morning. She should have known better than to trust the forecast.

Lex came up behind her. "What's wrong?"

She sighed. "I left my umbrella in the car."

He frowned and held out his hand. "Give me your keys, and I'll get it for you. Back seat?"

She considered arguing but didn't. She would prefer not to get drenched if she could avoid it. After giving him the keys, Joni watched as he dashed out the door and to her car. A minute later he was back. He handed her the umbrella.

"Thanks. Are you staying?"

"No."

She could take her umbrella and leave. After all, he couldn't have parked that far away. Lightning flashed across the sky, followed immediately by thunder. Incredibly it started to rain even harder. "Come on. I'll drop you at your car."

"Thanks."

Since Lex was several inches taller than her, Joni gave him back the umbrella. He held it in his right hand, and she grabbed his left arm. His bicep was firm beneath her fingers, reminding her of the strength she knew he had. They walked together to her car. He tried to guide her toward the driver's side, but she resisted. He'd already gotten drenched once. Once he was inside, she circled the car and got in. She started the engine, then turned to him. "Where are you parked?"

"City hall."

She should have known. Lex's dedication to the town was beyond anything that she'd ever seen. Sometimes she thought he worked too hard. But then, since she was equally dedicated to the success of the youth center, she wasn't in a position to judge.

After she let him out, she drove to work. Analisa had already opened the door. From the sound of it, there was a basketball game being played in the gym. Since it was raining, she expected more kids than usual would show up today.

She checked out the game for a few minutes, then went to her office to work on yet another grant proposal. Many corporations and private sponsors provided funding to youth programs. Filling out the paperwork required concentration; she needed to make sure that she followed the detailed instructions to the letter. Usually she had no trouble staying on task, but today was different. She couldn't quite focus, and she knew why.

Lex Devlin had hijacked her thoughts. He was slipping past her protective barriers and trying to worm his way into her heart. She couldn't let that happen. But short of keeping him out of her life, she didn't know how to stop it. And because of the baby, he'd always be in her life. Still, she had to fight hard. This was a battle she couldn't afford to lose. Not if she wanted to keep her heart intact.

Lex shut down his computer. He wasn't getting anything done, so it didn't make sense to sit here wasting time. He'd always been able to shut out the world and concentrate on work. It was that single-minded focus that had gotten him through the loss of his child seven years ago. Working long hours back then had helped to keep the pain manageable. Although the misery had dimmed with time and the pain no longer brought him to his knees, the ache had not totally gone away. Even now, all these years after Briana's death, he still felt her loss.

Now he was at risk for that kind of pain again. No matter how hard he told himself to be reasonable, how often he reminded himself that women had babies all the time, and that those babies lived more than four weeks and three days, he couldn't stem the worry that threatened to paralyze him. He was afraid for the baby Joni was carrying. Not only that, he was scared for Joni, too. She'd been so sick. What if her body wasn't strong enough to carry the baby? What if the morning sickness didn't pass? What if it was a sign of something worse?

Lex forced the thoughts away, refusing to let them gain control of him. Worrying wasn't going to change anything. At least, not for the better. It could drag him to that negative place he wanted to avoid.

Closing and locking his office door and then the city hall building behind him, he walked to his car. The rain had stopped, and the sky had cleared. The flowers in the pots that lined the streets were in full bloom, with a drop of moisture on a petal or two. Other than a few puddles, there was little evidence of the rain that had fallen a few hours ago.

Instead of driving straight to his empty house, he stopped by the youth center first. He didn't have a game scheduled with the kids, but he made a point to stop by the center on Saturday every once in a while to connect with the kids he missed during the week. He knew some kids came to the center because their home lives weren't the best. Mr. Harris and his cohorts had mentioned a couple of families they'd heard were struggling. Although the older men were usually the last to know things, this was the first Lex had heard of it. One of the families had a teenaged boy whom Lex had seen at the youth center. Lex intended to ask Joni about him, but he wanted a chance to talk to the kid himself first.

Joni's car was in the parking lot when Lex arrived, so he knew she was still there. Giving her the space she requested, he didn't stop by her office on his way to the gym. Six boys were playing three on three. Benji, the kid he was concerned about, was one of them. There were only a few minutes remaining on the game clock, so Lex leaned against the wall and watched them play. When the game ended, the players met at midcourt and shook hands before grabbing their bags from the bleachers. Benji didn't join them. Instead he dribbled the ball to the three-point line and shot it. Nothing but net.

"How about one more game?" Benji called to the other boys.

"Nah. I gotta get home. I'll see you next week," one of the boys responded as he walked out of the gym.

The other kids replied in similar fashion as they left, leaving Benji alone.

"I've got time," Lex said. "My clothes and shoes are in my trunk. Give me a couple of minutes to change."

The relieved smile on the young man's face nearly broke Lex's heart. Maybe the seniors were right about this kid's home life. Lex jogged to his car and grabbed his bag, then quickly changed. Benji was dribbling two balls when Lex returned. He passed one to Lex and set the other beneath a bench.

Lex took a practice shot from outside, then grabbed the rebound and went for a layup. "How about we play to twenty-one."

"Sounds good."

Lex checked the ball, and the two began a serious game of ball. They seemed evenly matched, and before long the score was tied at nine. Then Benji stole the ball and made a basket before Lex could even take a step. Then he did it again. Lex realized the kid had been toying with him. Lex was a good player, but Benji was outstanding. Fifteen minutes later the game was over with a score of twenty-one to eleven.

Lex looked at the teen, who wasn't even breathing hard. "You're good."

Benji grinned. "I was a starting guard on my high-school varsity team my freshman year. We moved to Sweet Briar in the middle of the season, so I didn't get a chance to play last year. I talked to the coach, and he said I should be a shoo-in this year. He knows some college recruiters, so he contacted them and invited them to come to some of the games, even though I'll only be a junior. If it all works out, I should get a college scholarship when I'm a senior."

"Where did you move from?"

"California. Twentynine Palms. My dad is—was a marine. We moved in with my mom's aunt after he died. Mom had been finishing college so she could become a teacher, but now she works as a waitress at Heaven on Earth."

Lex put his hand on the kid's shoulder. "I'm sorry for your loss. If there's anything you or your family need, let me know. If you don't think you know me well enough, ask someone you do feel comfortable talking to. We're all here and willing to help if you need anything."

"Thanks, Mayor. I'll keep that in mind."

Although it was getting late, Lex didn't want to end the afternoon on such a somber note. And they still had about fifteen minutes before the center closed. "Do you have time for one more game? I'd like to try and redeem myself."

The kid's face lit up. Lex had a feeling the kid would play all day and night if he could. The next game was a little tighter—twenty-one to sixteen, but Lex suspected that Benji was holding back. The kid was definitely gifted. Lex was looking forward to having him on his team for the battle of the sexes basketball tournament.

"Do you need a ride home?" Lex asked as they put the basketballs away and then turned off the gym lights.

"No, thanks. I have my bike."

The center was empty now, and their footsteps echoed through the hall as they walked to the front door. Joni's car was still in the parking lot, so after saying goodbye to Benji, Lex went back to Joni's office.

The door was closed, so he knocked. When he didn't get an answer, he opened the door and stepped inside.

Joni was sound asleep, her head on her desk and a pen in her hand. His heart seized with an emotion he wasn't sure he recognized or wanted to feel. He crossed the room and took the pen from her hand and placed it in the homemade pencil holder one of the kids had made for her. Ever so gently, he shook her shoulder. "Wake up, Joni. You need to get home."

"Lex?" Joni sighed but didn't open her eyes.

"Yes, it's me. Now it's time for you to wake up."

Joni gave a little moan, then her eyes opened. She straightened and sank back in her chair. When she finally focused on him, Lex read the confusion in her eyes.

"What time is it?"

"Three o'clock."

"Really? How long have I been asleep?"

Lex leaned against the corner of the desk and folded his arms. Apparently she wasn't concerned about the fact that she'd fallen asleep in the middle of the afternoon at her job, so maybe it wasn't a big deal. He certainly wasn't going to turn it into one by lecturing her about the importance of getting enough rest. "I don't know."

Joni stretched, then stood up. A moment later she wobbled, and he reached out a hand to steady her. She pushed it aside and ran from her office. He followed more slowly, knowing she was on the way to the ladies' room. When he reached the door, he stood outside knowing she wouldn't appreciate any interference from him. He tried to contain his worry, but it was a battle. How was his baby going to get any nourishment if Joni couldn't keep any food down?

The door swung open, and he made an effort to wipe all signs of concern from his face. "Better?"

Joni only grunted.

"I take that as a no."

"This morning sickness is getting old."

"Since it's the middle of the afternoon, I don't think it's morning sickness. Perhaps you should mention it to the doctor."

"I will. But according to the book you gave me, morning sickness is only the name. Some women are sick throughout the day." She made a face. "I guess I'm one of those lucky ones."

"Are you getting sick every afternoon?"

"Yes. That's one of the reasons I didn't realize I was pregnant. I figured I had caught that stomach bug that was going around."

Joni started to walk away, and he followed her. Instead of heading for her office, she started toward the back of the building.

He blocked her path. "Where are you going?"

"I need to make sure the building is secure before I leave."

"I can do that. Why don't you get your stuff together? I'll be back in a minute to walk out with you."

"You know what to do?"

"Of course." He'd accompanied her many nights while she'd closed the center. He knew her routine by heart. "I'll make sure all of the windows are closed and locked and put the chairs on the tables so the janitor can sweep and mop." They'd recently gotten the funds necessary to hire a janitorial service to come every night, so she and the volunteers no longer had to do heavy-duty cleaning.

"Don't forget to bring any forgotten books or jackets to me."

"I know." He began walking away.

"Be sure to adjust the room thermostats and close all of the doors."

He waved a hand to let her know he'd heard.

Ten minutes later he'd walked through every room and checked every window. Everything had been in order. When he got back to Joni, she'd cleared her desk. She looked up then grabbed her purse and put the strap over her shoulder.

"Everything is fine. Ready to go?"

"Yes."

Joni set the alarm, and they left. In the summer, the center was closed on Sundays, so Lex knew that she would have the day to rest. Joni pressed the key fob and unlocked her car door. Lex opened it immediately and held it for her. She smiled and slid inside.

"Call me if you need anything."

"I'll be fine. I think I need sleep more than anything right now."

Lex waited until Joni had driven off before he climbed into his car. For the first time since he'd moved to Sweet Briar, the thought of going home left him feeling lonely because nobody would be there when he arrived.

Chapter Seven

Monday morning Joni waved to a few kids as she walked through the youth-center parking lot. Analisa opened for her twice a week. Joni usually got to work on those days around nine o'clock or so, but today she just couldn't get her act together. She'd spent an easy day yesterday, sleeping or reading, which had her hoping that she'd manage to avoid the morning sickness today. Unfortunately that hadn't been the case.

"Hey, Ms. Joni. Do you want to jump rope with us?" Robyn called from the side playground. Ever since the younger girls had mastered double Dutch, they'd become fanatical about it and spent a good deal of time outdoors jumping rope. Since Joni liked the kids to get as much fresh air and exercise as they could, she was glad the girls had found an activity that interested them.

"Not right now. Thanks for inviting me."

"Okay. You can jump anytime you want. You won't even have to turn," Robyn promised.

"I'll keep that in mind," Joni said, then went inside.

The center was bustling as kids raced to their groups. Joni was invigorated by the activity. No matter what was weighing on her mind, being around the kids always uplifted her and gave her a new perspective. Nothing could keep her down long when she was with her kids.

Joni dropped her purse in her desk drawer, then walked around, making a point to speak to each volunteer and child. Several of the little ones hugged her. Although their greetings were nothing new, she felt tears well in her eyes as she returned their affectionate hugs. It wouldn't be long until her own child was wrapping his or her arms around Joni's waist. Joni hadn't planned on becoming a mother in this way, but she could hardly wait until her child was born.

Once she'd made her circuit, Joni went into the volunteers' lounge for a mug of tea. Arden came in just as she was adding a teaspoon of sugar to the drink. Joni smiled at her sister-in-law. "I didn't expect to see you here this morning."

"I didn't go with Brandon to the markets today, so I slept in. I was hoping to catch you before you left, but I must have missed you."

"Do you want to go to my office and talk?"

"It's nothing that requires privacy, so if you'd rather sit in here, I'm fine."

Joni pulled out a chair and sat down. A dozen single-serving bags of pretzels were piled in the middle of the table, and Joni grabbed and opened one. She pulled out a pretzel, dipped it into her tea and then popped it into her mouth. When she glanced up, Arden was looking at her with a raised eyebrow. "Why did you want to see me?"

Arden smiled. "Brandon and I are finally going on our honeymoon."

"That's great. When are you leaving, and where are you going?"

"We're leaving this Saturday. We're off to Paris for four weeks. We're going to take a couple of side trips to Italy and Spain. Maybe Switzerland if we have the time."

Joni grinned at the absolutely delighted expression on her sister-in-law's face. "Have a great time. The two of you deserve it."

"Thanks. I'm so excited. I hate to leave you short-handed here, especially with so little notice, but Brandon surprised me with the tickets last night. I can't believe he's actually going to leave the restaurant in someone else's hands for a whole month."

"That just goes to show how much he loves you."

Arden's smile turned dreamy. Joni had known from the minute she'd seen Brandon and Arden together that they were right for each other. She'd also predicted that her good friends Carmen and Trent would fall in love. Despite their rocky beginning, Joni had known that they would end up happily married. Joni was glad for both couples and wouldn't take away a minute of the joy they shared. She just wished there was someone who loved her the same way. Now that she was pregnant, she would have to put romance on the back burner. Her child had to come first in her life.

Besides, she couldn't even think about getting involved with anyone until she sorted out her feelings for Lex.

"I know. I love him just as much."

"I'll get your mail and take care of the house while you're gone."

"Thanks." Arden rose. "I knew we could count on you. I'd better get going. I have a thousand things to do before we leave. See you later."

After Arden left, Joni put a hand on her stomach. It looked like it was going to be just her and the baby. She thought of Lex and wondered if he would want to be there with them, then shook her head. He'd already given her his answer, and she had to live with it. "Don't worry, little one. We don't need anyone else. We're fine just as we are."

Joni spent the rest of the day with the kids. She made a pair of dangling earrings and a matching bracelet with some tween girls and then went outside where she joined a volleyball game for a few plays. When she spotted one of the younger girls on the playground struggling to set her swing in motion, Joni went over and offered to help. Lilia gave Joni a wide smile and nodded. Grabbing the chains, Joni took a couple of steps back and then let go. Lilia squealed in delight as she sailed over the grass, her chubby little legs pumping furiously to keep the swing in flight.

After watching to be sure Lilia had the hang of it, Joni sat on an empty swing and gave it a push. As she swung, the breeze blew in her face and lifted her hair from her neck. A minute later, Joni realized she'd made a mistake. The motion was making her nauseous. She dug her toe in the ground, jolting the swing into an abrupt stop. She closed her eyes and breathed deeply and slowly, waiting until the queasiness passed, before standing.

Telling Lilia goodbye, Joni went to her office. She'd intended to go to the store and pick up some ginger ale yesterday for moments just like this but had decided resting was more important. Tonight she'd stop at the store on the way home. She'd just turned on her computer when there was a knock on her open door. Eric, who was volunteering at the front desk today, held up a brown bag. "I have a delivery for you from Mabel's Diner."

"Delivery? Since when do they deliver?"

"Since the mayor gave one of the waiters a huge tip and asked him to bring this to you." He put the bag on her desk and smiled. "Judging from the grin on your face, I guess food is also the way to a woman's heart. Enjoy."

Eric was gone before she could correct him. Lex wasn't trying to win her heart. He'd already told her that he didn't want it. But he was smart enough to know that having lunch delivered was going to get him in her good graces. She pulled the food containers from the bag and opened them. A turkey sandwich, a bowl of chicken and rice soup and two large cups of ginger ale. Her smile broadened. This was one of the most thoughtful things anyone had ever done for her. But then, Lex had always been considerate. If he could help someone, he didn't hesitate, jumping in without being asked. He was always looking for opportunities to be a good neighbor. A good friend. And that was all he wanted them to be.

Joni grabbed the ginger ale and immediately took a sip. Her upset stomach began to settle.

Joni frequently worked and ate at the same time. Today she set aside her work and decided to enjoy her meal.

With every teaspoon of soup Joni swallowed, the warmth filled not only her stomach but her heart as well. The hurt and anger she'd been harboring toward Lex began to melt away. Oh, it wasn't totally gone. A special-delivery lunch, while sweet, only went so far. It couldn't totally remove the pain he'd caused her. Even though she now realized that she'd never really hated him, she still was disappointed in him and still angry. But she'd have to get over those feelings before the baby was born. She didn't want any negative feelings in her heart that she might inadvertently pass on to her child. Lex and their baby deserved to love each other with their whole hearts. That was clear to her.

If only her feelings for Lex were as clear. Unfortunately the anger and hurt and other negative feelings were in a constant battle with the longing and desire she felt. After the night they'd spent together, part of her heart had begun hoping for a different kind of relationship with Lex. She just wasn't sure if the feeling was real or the residue of a long weekend spent pretending to be in love, capped off by a night spent in each other's arms. And until she could distinguish fact from fiction, she was going to be fighting confusion as well as a myriad of other emotions.

Not that it mattered if her feelings were real. She already knew Lex didn't share them. Painful as that was to admit, Joni needed to face the truth in order to put the past behind her. She just wished it didn't hurt so much.

Putting down her spoon, she picked up her sandwich. It was prepared just the way she'd ordered it the other day. Lex must have been paying attention. Of course, Lex had always paid attention to details. Knowing that made her heart ache.

He was always so attuned to everything, so there was no way he'd missed how glorious she'd felt the morning after they'd made love. She'd all but floated on air. That was probably why the first words he'd uttered were of regret and apology. He'd wanted her to clamp down on her feelings before they had a chance to grow into something he didn't want to deal with.

It had worked and backfired all at once. The warm feelings that had filled her had turned cold. And all of the happiness had turned to sorrow and then hatred. Even as she acknowledged the hatred had vanished, she still had a lot of confusing feelings to work through. She still thought the best way to deal with them was to keep her distance from Lex, but that hadn't happened. He'd continued to come around. He'd been as charming as ever, but seemingly blind to the fact that her feelings of friendship had disappeared. Sometimes she wondered if he thought acting as if nothing had changed would make her forget that she was upset with him.

Never in her wildest imaginings had she thought Lex could be oblivious. Other men, sure. But Lex? She realized that she'd placed him on a pedestal. He'd been so perfect to her. Of course, that could be a result of their relationship being strictly platonic. She'd never considered him as anything other than a good friend, so she'd never scrutinized his behavior as a man. She'd never thought about what type of boyfriend he'd be. That one night had changed everything, including her expectations. She expected more of him than she ever had as a friend. And sadly he'd not lived up to her expectations. It might not be fair, but it was true.

Joni finished her lunch, and despite having spent most of the time wrestling with her thoughts, she suddenly felt energized. She needed to make a point of eating a good lunch at a reasonable time every day. When she'd been feeding only herself, it had been okay to grab a granola bar or apple on the run. Now that she was pregnant, she needed to take better care of herself.

That would be easier to do if her brother wasn't leaving town for a month. When Joni and Brandon moved to Sweet Briar, they'd lived together in his Victorian house. Being a chef, he'd renovated the kitchen to suit his needs. He loved cooking and had made all of their meals. She'd gotten spoiled. Even after Brandon and Arden had married and Joni had moved into the garage apartment, they often invited her to eat with them. She rarely did, preferring to give them their privacy. Now that she might wish to take them up on a couple of those invitations, they were going to be gone. Talk about bad timing.

Not that Joni couldn't cook. Even though her abilities didn't come anywhere near those of her brother, she did possess rudimentary skills. By necessity she was going to do more in her kitchen than warm up leftovers.

Joni tossed her trash, then got back to work. And truth be told, the warmth from Lex's thoughtfulness carried her throughout the rest of the day.

Lex answered the phone on the first ring, then settled more comfortably into his recliner.

"I hope I'm not disturbing you."

The sound of Joni's voice triggered instant desire in him, and he automatically shut it down. It was inappropriate to think of her in a sexual way. Thoughts led to actions, which in their case led to trouble. Given how distant she'd become since they'd made love, entertaining lustful thoughts was dangerous. Their friendship was too fragile for him to risk again.

He still couldn't believe how quickly everything had spun out of control that night. One minute they'd been congratulating themselves over how easily they'd convinced her friends and former fiancé that they were madly in love. Joni had been giddy with relief. They'd managed to get through four days of wedding festivities, including carriage rides, a backyard barbeque, the rehearsal dinner and finally the wedding and reception, without any of her friends becoming suspicious.

Andrea, the bride, had made all of the hotel arrangements. Since she'd believed Joni and Lex were involved, she'd booked a room with a king-size bed for them. There'd been a moment of awkwardness when they'd entered the room, since they'd expected to see two queen beds. It hadn't taken them long to decide it was silly to make a big deal out of sharing a bed. After all, they were best friends who'd never so much as kissed. Their relationship had never once come close to being sexual. And for four days and three nights that had remained true.

If they'd flown home after the reception, they'd still be good friends. But they hadn't. Instead they'd danced the night away. When they'd finally returned to their room, they'd both been relaxed. He still didn't know what had made him cross the line.

Was it the way the moonlight streaming through the window had illuminated her face? Or was it the way her bridesmaid's dress had caressed her fabulous curves? Or her soft scent that had teased him all night and had clung to his shirt? Whatever the reason, one minute they were toasting their success, the next they were wrapped in each other's arms and falling on the bed.

Wiping a hand across his suddenly damp forehead, Lex forced away the memories that had plagued him every night since then and focused on Joni's words.

"Of course you aren't disturbing me." At least not in the way she meant. "What's up?"

"I called to thank you for sending me lunch this afternoon. It really hit the spot."

"You're welcome. I know how busy you get." He was the same way, so he couldn't criticize her without being a hypocrite. But he couldn't allow her to get run-down. Having lunch delivered was something he could do without appearing heavy-handed.

"I appreciate it."

He didn't know what else to say, and apparently neither did she because a long silence stretched between them. Finally she said goodbye and hung up, bringing the awkward moment to a close.

He hated the way one night of passion had ruined a friendship that had lasted years. He'd always known the danger existed, which was the main reason he'd always resisted his attraction to Joni. He'd feared that sex would change, if not destroy, their perfect relationship. He'd been right. Nothing had been the same since that night. Now that Joni was pregnant, things could never go back to the way they'd been. He still hoped they could rebuild their friendship, but even if they couldn't, they had to find a way to go forward for the sake of their child.

After losing one baby, the thought of the child struck renewed fear in his heart. But underneath that fear was a joy at the idea of having a second chance to be a father. A chance to get it right. This time he would keep his child safe.

But he needed to know what to do and how to help. Caroline hadn't been sick one minute of her pregnancy. Joni was constantly sick. There were moments when she obviously was willing herself to keep going, but she wasn't her usual perky self. There had to be more he could do than send her soup and ginger ale. Although there were numerous books on pregnancy, and he'd done his share of reading over the past couple of days, the information they provided was general. He didn't need to know about a million women and their pregnancies. He needed to know about Joni's pregnancy. That's why it was imperative for him to go to her doctor's appointment with her.

Lex turned off the television. With all these concerns circling his mind, there was no way he was going to be able to follow the game. Lex was a big baseball fan. When he'd lived in New York, he and his brothers had season tickets, and they'd gone to games together. Suddenly he missed the old days when his brothers would drop over just to hang out.

Deciding to go for a ride, he hopped into his car. Though he had no particular destination in mind, he wasn't entirely surprised when he ended up standing on Joni's small porch. Before he could knock, the door swung open, and there she stood. She'd changed out of her work clothes and into a pair of blue satin pajamas. Her hair hung over her shoulders in a style that was at once casual and sexy. "What are you doing here?"

His voice failed him, and all he could do was shrug. He wanted to tell her that he'd missed her, but he didn't know how she would interpret that. The truth was he did miss her. Not just having her around, but the role she'd played in his life. She'd been not only his friend but his confidante. His constant companion. There was a hole in his heart that ached for her.

Joni opened the door wider, and he stepped inside. Immediately the loneliness vanished. "I just wanted to check on you."

Her brow wrinkled, and he knew she was confused. "We just talked a few minutes ago. You could have asked me then and saved yourself the trouble. As you can see, I'm fine."

"I needed to see for myself."

She sat down, and relieved that she wasn't going to throw him out, he followed suit. "Did you eat dinner?"

"Yes. I stopped by Heaven on Earth and grabbed a plate." She sighed. "I guess I won't be doing that for a while."

"Why not?"

"Brandon and Arden are finally taking a honeymoon. Marcus will be in charge of the restaurant while they're gone."

"So? He knows that you pick up dinner from time to time. As often as you help out, it's only fair."

"I know. But this is his first time running the restaurant for this long. I don't want him worrying about the boss's sister coming in unannounced, then reporting back to Brandon."

"Marcus doesn't strike me as the paranoid type."

"Maybe not. But I don't want to add to his stress. I don't want to do anything that could make him more nervous than he'll already be."

"That's very considerate of you. So what do you plan to do for meals?"

"I don't know. I guess I'll have to start cooking for myself."

Lex laughed. He'd never heard Joni sound so reluctant. Joni had many skills and interests, but cooking on a regular basis wasn't among them. Though the diner was good, she couldn't eat there every day of the week. There wasn't enough variety, and he didn't think it was healthy enough.

"I can help. I don't mind cooking. And I'm really good at it."

"So just what are you proposing here?"

"I'm proposing," he deliberately used her words, "that when you leave the youth center you come to my house where I'll cook for you. Or if you prefer, I can come here. Either way, I'll do the cooking, and you can relax."

"I don't want to put you out."

He managed not to smile. He knew she was protesting because she thought it was polite to do so. Or perhaps she still wanted to keep the distance between them. He hoped that wasn't the case, but even if it was, he knew she was going to agree to the arrangement. He'd be cooking dinner for Joni for the next four weeks. That would give him an opportunity to get close to her again.

Preparing meals together was nothing new. In the past, they'd cooked dinner together quite a lot. Or more accurately, he'd cooked while Joni had sipped a glass of wine and kept him company. Now the wine was out of the question, but he looked forward to enjoying the conversation.

"It's no problem. I have to cook dinner for myself anyway. It's no more work to cook for one more." Or one and a half, including the baby.

"Well, if you don't mind, then yes. Lately I'm really tired at the end of the day."

He'd read that being tired was normal, but his heart still stuttered with apprehension. Unless he found a way to get a handle on his fear, the next seven and a half months were going to be really long as he slowly went out of his mind.

Lex wanted to renew his request to accompany her to the doctor again but decided against it. He didn't want to chance Joni getting upset and then changing her mind about dinner. This whole walking-on-eggshells thing was a big change in their relationship. In the past no topic had been off-limits. There had been a freedom and comfort between them that he missed. Rebuilding that would take time, but it would be worth it.

"I'd enjoy it."

Joni covered a yawn. "Sorry."

"No need to apologize," Lex said. "You need to get your rest. I'll see you tomorrow."

Joni nodded, and they walked to the door together. They said good-night, then he jogged down the stairs to his car, feeling much more hopeful than he had only an hour ago. They'd made some progress tonight. He knew that they had a long way to go to become friends again. He just hoped he didn't blow it.

Chapter Eight

Joni gripped the clipboard holding the paperwork so tight her hands ached. She'd already filled out the insurance information and was waiting for the obstetric nurse to call her into the examination room.

"Hey," Lex said, easing the board from her fingers and setting it on his lap, "you're going to break this thing."

"I'm a little bit nervous." That was an understatement. She was scared out of her mind, although she didn't know why. She'd woken up this morning in a cold sweat. Fear had her blood racing through her veins at a ridiculous rate and her heart beating so hard she thought it might burst from her chest. In that moment she'd admitted the truth to herself. She didn't want to go to the doctor alone. She wanted someone with her. Since Lex already knew about the baby—

heck, he was the father—he was the logical choice. Besides, he wanted to come. Putting aside her pride, she'd called him.

He covered her hand with his. "Everything is going to be fine. You'll see."

"I know. I don't know why I'm so edgy."

"I can guess. Maybe it's because you've never been pregnant before and don't know what to expect."

Leave it to Lex to put her feelings into words. But then, he'd always been good at that. "Yes."

"Would you feel better if I went into the room with you, or would you prefer that I wait out here?"

"Out here."

Lex nodded, and Joni could see the disappointment in his eyes. She knew he wanted to be present during the exam, but that was just too intimate for her. Admittedly that thought didn't make a whole lot of sense. They'd made a child together, after all. But that night, she hadn't felt uncomfortable. Everything had been totally natural. Totally right. It was only the next morning, when he'd been filled with regret and had repeatedly apologized, that she'd been embarrassed. She'd been naked in more than just the physical sense. Her heart and soul had been laid before him, and he'd rejected them. Whenever she thought about that morning, she felt naked and raw. She wasn't ready to allow him to be with her when she would practically be naked. Not when she felt this vulnerable.

The nurse called her name, ending what was threatening to become one more awkward moment between them. Joni took the clipboard back from Lex. "This shouldn't take too long."

Joni followed the nurse, who'd introduced herself

as Sarah, down a brightly lit hall and into the exam room. Numerous baby pictures were pinned to a bulletin board under the words Special Deliveries. After instructing Joni to get into a gown, Sarah handed her a specimen cup and directed her to the ladies' room. Joni did as she was told and waited for the doctor to arrive. Fortunately the wait wasn't long.

Dr. Starkey entered the room and immediately introduced herself. She was about thirty-five, and her bright smile projected an air of confidence. "So, how have you been feeling?"

"I've had a lot of morning sickness. Sometimes it lasts until two or three in the afternoon."

"That happens. I suggest eating several little meals throughout the day. If necessary, keep fruit on your nightstand to eat if you wake up in the middle of the night. And if you can manage it, have breakfast in bed. Eating before you get up can help a lot."

Joni nodded and smiled, even though her heart fell. There was no one who could prepare breakfast for her. If Brandon and Arden weren't leaving, she might ask for their help. Brandon cooked breakfast most mornings. She lived steps away from their kitchen, so it wouldn't be too much of an inconvenience for someone to bring a tray to her apartment. But they were leaving to go on their long-delayed honeymoon. They would postpone their trip in a minute if they knew she needed their help, so she wouldn't tell them. She'd just have to figure out something else.

She immediately thought of Lex. He'd make breakfast for her in a heartbeat. But he was already going to cook dinner for her some nights. Even though she had no doubt he'd cook breakfast for her if she asked him, she wasn't ready to take that step. She didn't want to become even more dependent on him than she already was.

Dr. Starkey did a quick exam and then looked at Joni. "Any more questions?"

"I've been sick so much. Am I gaining enough weight? And is my baby getting enough to eat?"

"I wouldn't mind seeing you gain a few more pounds," the doctor said. "I think that will happen in time. And your baby is fine. Just keep taking the prenatal vitamins."

Joni nodded, relieved. She asked the doctor all of her questions, then went to the waiting room. When Lex saw her, he placed the magazine he'd been flipping through on the table and then joined her as she scheduled her next appointment.

"Everything okay?" Lex asked as they walked to the elevator.

"Yes. Everything is going according to schedule."

Lex heaved what could only be described as a sigh of relief. The fact that he was worried about her made her feel better than it should. She squashed that feeling and reminded herself that his concern was probably for the baby.

The elevator arrived, and they rode down in silence. Lex had gotten a parking spot near the entrance, so they didn't have far to walk. Joni had eaten a good breakfast, but a few hours had passed and she was getting hungry. With the hunger came nausea, something she wanted to avoid at all costs. She'd taken the entire day off, and Lex had cleared his calendar of all city business, so there was no need for them to hurry back to Sweet Briar.

Joni grabbed Lex's hand. "Do you mind stopping for lunch before we go back home?"

"Of course not. Do you have a taste for anything in particular?"

"You mean like a craving?"

He flashed her a grin. "Yes. Pickles and ice cream or some such."

"No. Sorry. I'm just hungry."

When they were in the car, Lex pulled onto the street. "You want to go to that steak place on Maple? You always liked their rib eye."

Joni nodded. She and Lex had come to Willow Creek many times over the years. She loved the people of Sweet Briar, but sometimes she wanted to get away to a place where she was less likely to run into the parents of the kids she worked with. A place where people wouldn't just come up to Lex to complain about garbage pickup or the kinds of flowers in the planters on Main Street.

Lex turned the radio to a station that played a mixture of old school and new school. The station was a compromise because they had such different tastes in music. Right now they were playing a classic. Lex tapped his fingers on the steering wheel and hummed along with the lead singer. Joni rolled her eyes and hoped the next song would be something more to her liking.

Most of the lunchtime diners were finishing their meals by the time Joni and Lex reached the restaurant, so they only needed to wait a few minutes before they were shown to a table. After requesting drinks—lemonade for Joni and a cola for Lex—they studied their menus. Joni's stomach growled, and she was glad that they had decided to stop and eat. When the waitress returned with their beverages, they placed their orders. Joni took a sip of her drink, then leaned back in her chair.

They hadn't talked much today, and when they had, their conversation had been limited to small talk. Joni knew she had to make a more concerted effort to be friendly. She needed to put past hurt behind her if they were going to have a good relationship again. And they needed to have a good relationship.

Joni's parents had been married for over thirty-five years, and they still behaved like newlyweds. In her teens, Joni had been embarrassed to walk into a room and catch her parents in a clinch. Now she appreciated the love and affection that her parents had modeled. Joni had hoped to demonstrate that same kind of love and devotion for her children as well. That wasn't going to happen now, but it didn't mean her relationship with Lex had to be strained. She certainly didn't want it to be. That wouldn't be good for their child.

Lex had more than held up his end—even in the face of her resistance. He'd been the one to make the effort, seeking her out at the diner, coming to the youth center, or sending her a meal, even accompanying her to the doctor at a moment's notice. Perhaps she needed to take the initiative this time and open up the conversation. It used to be so easy. Maybe if they both tried, things between them could become easy again.

"Do you want a son or a daughter?" Joni asked.

Lex looked at her with surprise. Was the look because she'd been the one to start the conversation? Or was it because she'd mentioned the baby? He smiled.

"I don't have a preference. As long as he or she is healthy, I'll be happy."

"So you haven't been picturing yourself running up and down the basketball court with a son, teaching him how to dunk?"

"Ha. The way the teenagers have been whipping me in our games, I'll be lucky to be able to walk down the court by the time this one is old enough to play."

"It's not you, Lex. It's your teammates. You've still got it." He grinned wolfishly, and her face immediately heated. She hadn't meant that to sound as flirtatious as it had come out. Needing to cool the heat that was suddenly between them, she added, "Well, for an old guy."

"Forty is the new thirty."

"Maybe." She smiled and tossed her hair over her shoulder. "But lucky for me twenty-nine doesn't have to be the new anything."

"You've got me there. I'll just have to do my best to keep up."

Keeping up had never been Lex's problem. And though he'd been joking, he really did have the build and stamina of a man of thirty. Apart from his desire to listen to music of another millennium, his mind-set was modern. She knew he'd never turn into that cranky old man yelling at kids to stay off his lawn. Heck, he'd probably ask them if he could play.

"I'm sure you'll do fine. Not to mention that you'll have so much wisdom to impart. I see the way the kids come to you for advice. You have a way with them."

"I'm not any wiser than their parents. I probably say the same things as their fathers. It's just that I'm not their parent, so it's easier for them to listen to me.

They'd probably be happy with any other man's perspective."

"Maybe. But I don't see them going to Trent the way they go to you."

Lex laughed. Though Trent had relaxed some since marrying Carmen a few years back, he still had a black-and-white view of the world. "True."

The waitress returned with their meals, and they continued to discuss the baby and the hopes they held for him or her. Each of them had grown up in loving homes with parents who'd always supported them, and they wanted to give their child the same. Listening to Lex, Joni could hear the love he already had for their unborn baby. She and Lex weren't in love, so she couldn't claim her child had been created in love, but she had no doubt their baby would grow up surrounded by love.

Lex regaled her with stories of how he'd grown up. Some she'd heard before, but others were new to her. Most were funny, but all shared an underlying feeling of affection. Even if she couldn't provide the dream family and the white picket fence, Joni would be able to give her baby a loving extended family.

After they'd finished eating, Lex insisted that they sit for a while just to be sure that Joni didn't get sick. She tried to explain to him that morning sickness didn't work that way, but he was so worried that she didn't argue. Once he was satisfied that Joni would be able to ride home without risking morning sickness, car sickness, or anything else his suddenly overactive imagination came up with, he settled the bill and they left.

Lex took Joni's hand as they walked to the car. Suddenly overwhelmed with joy, Joni stopped, stood on her tiptoes and kissed his cheek.

"What was that for?"

"I don't know. I'm just feeling happy."

Lex's grin was decidedly rakish. "So am I."

She knew what he intended, and if she wanted to, she could have stepped away. Instead, heart pounding, she waited for his kiss.

The instant his lips brushed hers, electricity shot through her body. She stepped closer into his arms, willing him to deepen the kiss. He did for a moment, then he pulled back, leaving her yearning for more. Blowing out a breath, she pushed the desire away. There wouldn't be anything romantic between them. She needed to remember that.

Lex drove back to Sweet Briar, replaying the kiss in his mind. He'd been surprised when Joni kissed him. It would have been wiser for him to have let the moment end there. But no, he'd given in to his passion. Luckily he'd gotten control of himself before things got out of hand. Still, he had to do better in the future. He couldn't take any more unnecessary risks.

He was still furious with himself for damaging their relationship. For a while it had looked like the rift would be permanent. Thanks to the baby she was carrying, they would always have a connection. Not that he would use the baby to stay close to Joni. He loved this baby for him- or herself. Still, the baby made it essential for him and Joni to get along. And it gave him hope that with enough time they could become close again.

When they reached her block, he pulled into her

driveway. He'd never considered anything wrong with her garage apartment, but now he thought it was too small for her and a child. Eventually she was going to have to move. He'd grown up with plenty of space, so he couldn't imagine any less for his child. His house, though not ostentatious, had four bedrooms and three baths and sat on an acre of land. There was more than enough room for their child to run and play.

Maybe he could convince Joni to move in with him. As soon as the idea popped into his mind, he dismissed it. Joni wasn't going to agree to that. She was independent and quite capable of purchasing a house of her own if she wanted one. Although she didn't make a huge salary, he knew Brandon didn't charge her much rent. In fact, that had been a bone of contention between brother and sister. She'd wanted to pay rent, but since she helped at the restaurant without taking a salary, he'd refused to take her money. They'd finally agreed on a token amount. Even though she often purchased items for kids at the youth center, she'd been able to save a majority of the money she'd earned over the past years. And if she didn't have enough money to buy the house she wanted, Lex would make up the difference. He had no intention of being a deadbeat dad. He'd make sure Joni and his child had whatever they wanted.

Joni had fallen asleep on the ride, and he took a moment to look at her before he woke her up. She really was beautiful. Her face and body were perfection. Not that her looks were the most important qualities or even her most attractive. She possessed a pure spirit. The kindness and sweetness she showed to one and all could never be matched, even by high cheekbones, full lips and clear brown eyes.

Joni sighed, and Lex shook himself out of his stupor. He could look at her for hours on end and never get tired, but he knew he wasn't doing her any favors by letting her sleep sitting up. She needed to get in bed so that she could be comfortable. Even knowing that, he was reluctant to wake her and bring their time alone together to an end. But it was the right thing to do.

"Joni," he whispered. He leaned close to her, and her tantalizing scent surrounded him. Lex was accustomed to being around women who smelled good, but none of them had even come close to smelling as good as Joni. There was something about her scent that threatened to bring him to his knees. It was more than the perfume he'd had designed especially for her. It was her own very unique scent that he found addictive.

Stirring, Joni opened her eyes. He could tell she was still half-asleep. "Lex."

"Yep."

She smiled. "I was just dreaming about you."

"Were you? And do I want to know what the dream was about?"

She blinked, shook her head and sat up as she came the rest of the way awake. "What did I just say?"

"That you were dreaming about me."

She frowned and moved away from him. Since they were in the car, she couldn't move very far. Still, those inches felt like miles. The mood in the car had shifted from fun to stilted in under five seconds. Recognizing that there was nothing he could do to change things back, Lex got out and circled the car to open her door.

They were standing beside the car when Brandon and Arden emerged from their house.

"Hey," Brandon called as he and his wife approached. "What are you guys doing here at this time of day?"

Joni looked at Lex with panicked eyes. Clearly she couldn't think of a response. He knew she didn't want to reveal her pregnancy just as he knew she'd never knowingly lie to her brother. Lex wouldn't lie either, but he wouldn't tell Brandon and Arden something Joni didn't want them to know yet. "We took the day off. We just got back from lunch in Willow Creek. So, you two are finally taking that honeymoon."

Arden and Brandon exchanged happy smiles. "We're leaving first thing in the morning."

"I hope you have a great time," Lex said. "I can tell you were on your way out, and I don't want to keep you."

"Thanks. We have one last run to make." Brandon reached over and pulled Joni into a hug. "That's in case I don't get to say goodbye later."

"You guys have fun." Joni returned her brother's hug before hugging her sister-in-law.

"And even though I know she's grown and stubborn as heck," Brandon said, "I'm asking you to look out for her while we're gone."

"I'm perfectly capable of taking care of myself," Joni replied.

"Like I said. *Stubborn*," Brandon said.

"Don't worry," Lex replied. "I'll be here in case Joni needs anything, so the two of you can enjoy your honeymoon."

Joni and Arden rolled their eyes. Lex knew that

under ordinary circumstances Joni could take care of herself. But since Lex knew that Joni was having a difficult pregnancy, he'd use this promise to Brandon to make sure that Joni had all that she needed.

Joni didn't go inside her apartment after Brandon and Arden drove away. Instead she stared into space. The sun was shining, and there was a nice breeze, but Lex didn't think she was stopping a moment to take in the beauty of the day. He knew Joni well enough to know that there was something going on beneath the surface. But he also knew that she wasn't going to say anything until she was good and ready. Lucky for him, he didn't have anything on his agenda for the rest of the day, so he had all the time in the world.

Eventually Joni turned and smiled at him, and his heart sank as he realized that she wasn't going to share whatever had made her so pensive. He could mourn their lost closeness, but that wouldn't change anything. It was time to get over their past relationship. It was dead, and he needed to bury it. Only then would they be able to build a new one. It might not be like what they would have had if he hadn't lost control, but it was the only relationship they were going to get.

"Well. I guess I'll say goodbye. Thanks for taking me to the doctor. I'll see you around."

"You'll see me again in a few hours. Remember, I'm making dinner for you."

"That's not necessary. Carmen and Trent invited me tonight."

He could finagle an invitation but decided against it. If Joni had wanted him to come, she would have asked him. Maybe she needed some time with a girl-friend. "Okay. Enjoy yourself."

He waited until she'd climbed the stairs and gone inside her apartment before he drove off. They couldn't keep going around in circles. It was time to get things moving in a different direction.

Chapter Nine

Exhausted, Joni dropped into her chair. She hated to admit it, but she was looking forward to Lex cooking dinner for her tonight. It had been three days since Brandon and Arden had left, and she missed them. But it wasn't just them she missed. She missed Lex.

Though they'd agreed that he would cook dinner for her occasionally, she'd been putting him off. First she'd had dinner with Carmen and Trent. Then she'd used the weekend as an excuse to keep him at a distance. Since she only worked a couple of hours on Saturday and none on Sunday, she'd told him she could handle dinner on her own. And she had.

But she hadn't counted on how lonely those dinners would feel. Whether she ate at the breakfast bar or sitting on the couch with the television on in the background, she couldn't shake the loneliness that draped over her like her grandmother's shawl. It had taken her a minute, but she'd finally admitted that she longed for Lex. There was an empty place in her heart that he alone had been able to fill. And that was too bad because he didn't want a place in her heart. Somehow she was going to have to accept that and find another way to fill that hole.

But not today. Today she was tired and hungry. Besides, she didn't think Lex would take no for an answer again as he had this weekend.

The inaugural Sweet Briar Youth Center Olympics had started today with great fanfare. She'd been looking forward to this day for a while. Of course, when she'd planned the event four months ago, she hadn't known she would be pregnant. Although she had a wonderful team of volunteers, she was responsible for ensuring that the entire week of activities, which culminated with a closing ceremony on Friday, was a success.

The opening ceremonies had included several high-school bands and cheering squads from as far as an hour away leading the parade down Main Street. Each athlete who wanted to march had been allowed to. The youngest participants beamed from ear to ear as they'd carried banners or posters they'd made in art class. When the parade ended, the events had begun in earnest.

Joni had spent the day running from competition to competition, helping to keep the games on schedule. She'd handed out medals to the winners and certificates to every participant. Although the games had only lasted three hours, there had also been lunch to supervise. She was tired beyond belief, but today had been a success. If the rest of the week went as well, she would be thrilled.

Not that she took all or even most of the credit.

Part of making any event a success was buy-in from the kids. If they didn't want to participate, then it would be a bust no matter how much work went into planning. She'd never doubted that the little kids would be enthused, but she'd worried about the older kids. Fortunately the teens had been on board from the beginning. They'd even created some of the competitions. The speed puzzle-finishing game, which had been a big hit, had been the idea of a group of teens. They'd done all the work required, including writing the rules, making the jigsaw puzzles and refereeing. There had been much laughter and cheering, which spurred the little ones to finish the game. Suzanne Martin, one of the quieter kids, had been the winner. She'd smiled so brightly as her gold medal had been draped around her neck that Joni's eyes had filled with tears.

As happy as she'd been for Suzanne and all of the competitors, she was even more thrilled by the participation of the teenagers. Although their games wouldn't be held until later in the week, they'd come out in great numbers to support the little kids. They'd cheered as each child was introduced, and some even took pictures with their phones that Joni would frame and hang on the walls. Their support had meant so much to the younger kids who looked up to the teens. It warmed Joni's heart to see the older ones looking out for the younger ones.

That, to her, was evidence that the youth center was really serving its true purpose. Sure, a big part of the youth center's mission was to provide the kids with a safe place to learn skills and have fun. The art and computer classes were very popular. The sports were as well. But more than being a supervised location, the center was charged with helping the youth become well-rounded adults. And part of that involved letting them be in charge of activities that encouraged them to support the younger kids. And it was working.

But her job as director required her to be a role model, too. She knew many of the teen girls emulated her. They frequently sought her out for advice on a wide variety of topics, ranging from schoolwork and bullying to fashion and, of course, boys. She'd done her best to guide them in the right direction and to help them stay on track so they could live up to their potential and reach their goals.

And now she was pregnant. How would that play out with parents? The people of Sweet Briar were generally accepting and nonjudgmental, but that didn't mean they'd think an unwed mother was the best person to run the youth center. And since marriage wasn't on the horizon for her, she'd be unwed when her baby arrived.

She'd never pretended to be perfect. And though her child hadn't been planned, she didn't think of her baby as a mistake. Certainly the citizens of this town could distinguish between a gainfully employed, educated woman and a high-school teenager getting pregnant. If not? She might have to come up with a plan B for her life.

A knock on her door interrupted her thoughts before they could travel down that road. Looking up, Joni smiled at Analisa.

"Joni, I just wanted to let you know that everything is all set for tomorrow. I closed and locked all of the rooms, so you don't have to."

"Thank you. You are a lifesaver."

"No problem. There are kids in the gym playing ball, but Eddie and Steve are in there with them. They're going to lock up tonight."

Joni nodded. Eddie and Steve were cousins and two of her favorite volunteers. One was a sheriff's deputy, and the other was a firefighter. She knew the kids and the center would be in good hands tonight.

"Thanks, Analisa. You did a great job today. Every day, really. I appreciate all that you do."

Analisa beamed. "Thank you. I love my job. See you tomorrow."

"See you."

Joni had about an hour of work to do before she left, so she popped a mint into her mouth and got busy.

"Hey, Joni, ready to go?"

Joni looked up from her pad. Although she used her computer to complete a lot of tasks, she used a pen and yellow legal pad for brainstorming. Her mind seemed to come up with her best ideas when she worked the old-fashioned way. "Hey, Lex. I wasn't expecting you until about six."

"It's six fifteen."

"Oh. Wow." Almost an hour had passed. She looked at her pad. She'd come up with some great ideas. Then she yawned.

"You're exhausted."

"Not really. That just came out of nowhere."

He was looking at her dubiously. Given the fact that he'd caught her sleeping at work recently, she knew she wouldn't be able to convince him, so she didn't bother trying.

"Why don't you let me drive you home tonight? I'm coming over anyway to cook dinner for you. That way you can rest. If you're up to it, I'll bring you back tonight to get the car. If not, I'll drop you off in the morning."

"Once the air hits me I'll be fine." She tossed some files she needed to review into her purse.

"Okay, but I'm following you."

She nodded. He was coming to her apartment anyway. They walked out of the center together and got into their separate cars.

The ride home was fast, and before long she was pulling into her driveway, Lex's car right behind hers. He grabbed a bag of groceries from his trunk, and they went up the stairs.

"Do you mind if I take a shower?" Joni asked when they were inside her apartment. "I'm sort of sticky."

"Go ahead. I stopped by the center just in time to see you get an ice cream cone right down the front of your shirt. And you were hugged by quite a few sticky hands."

"And patted on the legs. Not to mention the spilled drinks." And she'd done a lot of sweating running from event to event in the hot sun. Still, everyone had enjoyed themselves immensely, so it had all been worth it.

"Dinner won't be ready for about a half an hour, so take your time."

Joni went into the bathroom and pulled off her clothes as fast as she could, then stepped under the warm water. Her skin began to tingle as the stickiness was washed off. She used her favorite scented body wash to get clean, and then despite how good the water felt, she stepped out of the shower. After she dried off, she wrapped herself in a fluffy line-dried towel and looked around. In her haste to get out of the uncomfortable shorts and T-shirt, she'd forgotten to bring clean clothes into the bathroom with her.

Now what? She looked at the hamper where she'd just placed her dirty clothes. There was no way in the world she was going to put on those sticky things again. Which meant one thing. She was going to have to go to her bedroom wearing only a towel.

Instead of opening the door and walking into her bedroom where her clothes were, she stared at the bathroom door. Knowing Lex was on the other side kept her feet glued to the cool marble. It wasn't until she began to shiver that Joni twisted the doorknob and opened the door.

The apartment was small, so even though the bathroom didn't open directly onto the kitchen, if Lex looked up when he heard the door open, which she expected he'd do reflexively, he'd catch a glimpse of her before she reached her bedroom.

Deciding she was making way too big a deal of this, she stepped into the hallway. She thought Lex was still in the kitchen, but she was wrong. He was in the hallway, mere inches away from her. Apparently he'd finished his meal prep and was on his way to the living room. When he saw her, he froze. His eyes traveled over her body, heating her skin as if his hands had actually touched her.

Her mouth went dry, and she found herself searching for words that wouldn't come. Sexual tension suddenly filled the air, and Joni felt her chest rise and fall as her breathing became shallow. Her legs grew weak, and she didn't know how much longer they would hold her up. Then Lex blinked as if emerging from a spell and stepped aside.

"Go ahead." His voice, low and gritty, sent Joni scurrying to her room on shaky legs.

Once inside, she closed the door and leaned against it. *Whew.* Her skin, which she'd toweled dry, was damp with perspiration. She dragged the fabric over her body and then hastily put on the first thing she got her hands on, a summer dress. It was made of a light cotton and stopped a couple of inches above her knees. It would definitely keep her cool, no matter how many heated glances Lex sent her way.

Not that Lex had done or said anything inappropriate. Truth be told, he'd been a perfect gentleman. She was the one whose imagination was running wild and whose hormones had shifted into overdrive. So she was the one who needed to get control of herself, preferably before she did something outrageous, like flirt. They were about to be parents together and were doing their best to become friends again. The last thing they needed was sexual attraction complicating matters. After all, it was giving in to that attraction that had gotten them into this mess in the first place. Joni wasn't going to make the same mistake twice. The consequences would be too severe.

Lex waited until the door closed behind Joni before daring to move. Blowing out a deep breath, he fought to gain control of his body. The last time he'd given in to his desire had been catastrophic. No, that wasn't accurate. Making love to Joni had been earth-shattering in the best possible way. It was only after his mind had cleared and he'd realized what he'd done that his world had begun to collapse. He couldn't make that mistake again.

He went back into the kitchen. Not that there was anything he needed to do here. The chicken breasts and cream of mushroom soup were bubbling in the pan on the stove. The rice was cooking, and the broccoli crowns were washed and ready to be steamed. He'd already put two place settings on the breakfast bar that separated the kitchen from the living room. The only thing for him to do was pace, which is what he did. It was either take four steps from one end of the kitchen and back or knock on Joni's door and beg for affection like a dog. Knowing it would be a mistake didn't lessen the urge or diminish the appeal of spending some quality time with Joni in her bed.

"You're an idiot," he muttered.

"Talking to yourself? That's the first sign that you're losing your mind."

Lex spun around and stared at Joni. One look at her was enough to take his breath away. She was just so beautiful. Although he appreciated her kind heart, that didn't stop him from noticing how sexy and desirable she was. Looking at her now, everything male in him jumped to attention, and it was a struggle not to take her into his arms. It was a second before her words penetrated his brain. When they did, he smiled. "Maybe. But since I live alone, there's nobody to tell on me."

Joni pointed at her chest. "But you're not alone now.

And even though I couldn't understand what you said, I definitely witnessed my mayor talking to himself."

"You got me there."

Joni stepped all the way into the kitchen, closing the distance between them. The room was tiny to begin with, and with both of them in it, there wasn't much space to maneuver. Not that he wanted more distance between them. He liked being close enough to feel the heat from her body. And nothing could ever be as good as inhaling her sweet scent. Even when she'd been her angriest and most disappointed in him, she'd continued to wear the perfume he'd created for her. He inhaled and knew that she'd dabbed a bit behind her ears today.

"What are you making?" Joni lifted the lid on the pot, and steam floated on the air.

"It's the chicken and soup you like so much."

"How much longer until it's done?"

"Not long. Maybe ten or so minutes."

"I'm starving." She picked up an orange and started to peel it.

"That's a good sign."

"Of what?"

"That the baby is healthy."

She put one hand on her stomach. "It's hard to believe that I'm pregnant. I still look the same. If it wasn't for this awful morning sickness, I'd think it was all a figment of my imagination."

"Would you prefer not to be pregnant?" He held his breath while waiting for her response.

"No. It was totally unplanned and unexpected, but now that I know there's a baby growing inside me, I'm happy about it." She put a couple of orange slices into her mouth and chewed slowly. "Of course, I would be so much happier if I didn't spend so much of my day feeling nauseous. That's definitely something I can do without."

"Is it getting any better?"

She polished off the rest of the orange before answering. "Not really. Dr. Starkey told me that the second trimester is usually better, so hopefully all of this will be a memory in a few more weeks."

Lex hoped so, too, but he knew there was a slim possibility that the morning sickness could continue well into the second trimester. Heck, she could be one of those rare women who was sick throughout her pregnancy. The thought sent chills down his spine, and he struggled to rid himself of the worry. There was no sense borrowing trouble.

When dinner was ready, Lex sent Joni to sit down, then fixed their plates. They'd eaten many meals together, but tonight felt like the first time. Perhaps because after weeks of being banished from her home and longing for her company, they were once again side-by-side at her breakfast bar.

Joni scooped up bits of chicken and rice and grinned at him. "Don't tell Brandon, but this is my absolute favorite meal. I don't think his ego could take it."

Lex laughed. "No worries. It'll be our secret."

"We seem to have quite a few of them these days."

Joni suddenly sounded sad, so he set down his fork and looked at her. "How does that make you feel?"

"I hate it."

"We can always tell people about the baby."

"I'm not ready yet."

"Okay. You're the one in charge. I'll do whatever you want. You just have to let me know what that is."

Her eyes filled with tears, and she blinked rapidly. He hadn't meant to upset her and was in the middle of an apology when she held up a hand. "Stop. I'm not upset. I told you before it's just the hormones."

"Do they make you just start crying for no reason at all?" He didn't recall Caroline's pregnancy being that way. But then, he'd done his best to forget everything related to that painful time surrounding Briana's death.

She dabbed at her eyes. "No. It's just that you're being so understanding about everything."

"Oh, Joni. You're the one doing everything. You're sick and nauseous all because you're pregnant with our child. Nothing I do will ever compare to that. I don't deserve credit for being understanding. You deserve nothing less."

He'd spoken from his heart, but perhaps he hadn't adequately reflected the depth of his emotion, because her tears really began to fall. Deciding that words weren't working at the moment, Lex wrapped his arm around Joni's shoulder and led her to the living room. He helped her to sit on the sofa, then sat beside her.

Holding her close, Lex whispered comforting words, hoping that they would help. But since he had no idea what she was thinking or feeling, he felt inadequate. Once they'd known each other so well they hadn't needed words. They'd been able to sense each other's feelings. It was as if they'd shared one mind. They'd often laughed at how in tune they were with each other. Ever since that night, he'd lost the ability to know what she thought or felt. He missed that connection and wished he knew how to get it back.

But he was coming to believe there wasn't a way. It appeared that the damage he'd done was too deep to overcome. As much as he hated the idea, it might be best to get used to the new relationship that he and Joni had. His heart rebelled at the idea. With Joni carrying his child, they needed their special kind of communication back more than ever. He was just going to have to try harder. After all, hard work and dedication could achieve just about anything.

Once her tears slowed, Lex pulled back so he could look into her eyes. "Better?"

"Yes."

"Good. Do you want to finish your dinner? I can warm it up if you want."

"No. I had enough for now. I think I'll go lie down for a while."

"Okay. You do that, and I'll put away the leftovers and take care of the dishes."

"Thanks."

Lex watched as Joni left the room. He sat on the couch for a while before he got up. His appetite gone, he covered their plates with foil, put the food from the pots into containers, put them all in the refrigerator and then cleaned the kitchen. Worried about Joni, he returned to the living room and turned on the television. He found a baseball game and settled back. He'd watch until he was sure Joni was asleep for the night before going home.

Lex watched the game, and when it ended he tiptoed into Joni's bedroom. Once inside, he took a moment to just look at her. She was sleeping so peacefully, and her face looked so very young. Her hair was spread over her pillow, and his mind flashed back to that night weeks ago. Unable to stop himself, he reached out and caressed her cheek. Her skin was just as soft and warm as he remembered. Sometimes he thought he might have been exaggerating the memory, but he hadn't been. If anything, he'd underplayed it. Or the power that the simplest contact had. Desire was pulsing along with the blood in his veins, and Lex reluctantly removed his hand.

The sheet Joni had been lying beneath had become twisted around her legs, so he straightened it and covered her with it. Having no further reason to stay in her room, Lex backed out. He checked to make sure the stove was off, then left, locking the door behind him.

He got in his car and drove home, feeling inexplicably lonely. He then comforted himself with the knowledge that he would see Joni again in the morning. Surely he could hold out that long.

Chapter Ten

Joni leaned her head against her bathroom wall and wiped her hand across her forehead. She'd hoped that she would get over her morning sickness, but that hadn't happened yet. Thankfully it was Saturday and she could crawl back into bed. She hoped the doctor was right, and the second trimester would be better, because there was no way she would survive otherwise. Not that she thought she would die from being sick. Even at her most imaginative, she didn't think that.

Her mind flashed back to what the doctor had told her about starting her day with breakfast in bed, and she began to laugh. It wasn't a happy laugh, and it soon turned to tears. Joni didn't try to stop the tears from falling. Instead she began to sob. She'd never felt so alone in her life. Even when Darrin had told her that he'd been cheating on her with one of her sorority sisters, she hadn't felt so lonely. She'd been devastated, but she'd had her family and friends to turn to. They'd been a rock for her.

But that wasn't the case now. Her family and friends didn't know about the baby. The only person who knew was Lex, and she didn't want to lean on him any more than she already had. She knew that way of thinking wasn't logical. He was her child's father, after all. But she couldn't risk her heart. She was already emotional and subject to the whims of her hormones. It would be too easy to confuse his concern for her well-being with something else. Something romantic. Something that didn't exist. And then where would she be? Devastated once more. Letting Lex further into her life when she had barely put the pieces of her heart back together would be stupid. Those feelings that had led her to make love with him would only grow and become harder to control.

Joni heard her front door open, quickly followed by footsteps. She moved to close the bathroom door, but it was too late.

"Joni? Are you sick again?" Lex was by her side before she could answer. He put one arm under her knees and the other around her waist and picked her up. "Let's get you back into bed."

She longed to rest her head on his shoulder and absorb his strength, but she squelched that desire and pushed against his chest. "I need to brush my teeth."

Although he let go of her knees so she could stand, he kept an arm around her waist. Allowing herself a moment of weakness, she leaned against him before putting toothpaste on her toothbrush and quickly brushing her teeth. When she was done, Lex scooped her into his arms and carried her to bed. It felt good to be in his arms, and for a ridiculous minute she wished the distance between her bathroom and bedroom was greater.

After he'd set her down, he pulled the sheet up to her waist, then sat beside her. "Did you tell the doctor how sick you've been?"

"Yes."

"What did she say? Surely there has to be something you can do."

Joni ducked her head, suddenly unwilling to meet Lex's eyes. She felt a gentle finger on her chin, lifting her face until she was once more eye to eye with him. Joni sighed. "There is something she suggested might work."

"What's that?"

The concern she saw in his eyes filled her with guilt and shame. It was foolish to let her silly pride over-rule her common sense. Lex only wanted to help her. And she did need help. "She said I should eat breakfast in bed."

"Why didn't you say anything?"

"I didn't want to ask you," she confessed. "You've cooked dinner for me every day this week. I didn't want to take advantage of you." He'd waited for her and then followed her home each night after the Sweet Briar Olympics and cooked while she'd showered and dressed. After the first awkward evening, she'd re-membered to bring her clothes into the bathroom with her. Last night she'd been too tired to drive, so she'd left her car in the lot. Since today was Saturday, she and Lex could pick it up anytime.

He wiped his hand down his face, a sign that he was angry or frustrated and trying to gain control of himself before speaking. Clearly the fight not to speak in anger was a bigger struggle than Joni had anticipated. Could he actually be that upset? Finally he looked at her. The anger she expected to see in his eyes was missing. Instead he only looked sad. "I don't mind cooking for you. There's nothing I won't do for you. You used to know that."

A part of her still did. "I just hoped it would pass."

"And has it?"

She shook her head.

"What were you planning on eating this morning?"

"I hadn't thought about it."

"Give me a few minutes, and I'll fix something. Would you like some tea while you wait?"

"Please."

As Lex walked out, Joni was filled with remorse. She'd really hurt his feelings. It didn't matter that hurting Lex was the last thing she'd ever want to do and that it was totally unintentional. The result was the same. He was hurt. All because she wanted to protect her own heart. And she still did. But she didn't want to break his in the process.

One thing had become abundantly clear. She finally believed that Lex hadn't intended to hurt her. Sure, she'd told herself that more than once. But now she not only knew it, she felt it. Causing her pain had been painful to him as well. Just as she was suffering now because she knew how badly she'd hurt him. She didn't know what to do with this knowledge. Perhaps she didn't need to do anything. Maybe knowing was enough.

A minute later Lex returned carrying a mug of tea and a few saltines on a saucer. He moved a book from her nightstand and put the mug and saucer there. "I figured you could use some crackers, too. Breakfast will be ready in fifteen minutes."

Joni reached out and grabbed his hand. "Thank you, Lex. I appreciate it."

"It's not a big deal, Joni." His voice was sharp.

"Still, I want to let you know that I'm grateful for everything that you're doing for me. There was a time when telling you that wouldn't make you angry."

Lex laughed. "You're right. I guess I'm being hypersensitive."

"That's understandable. This is a new situation for both of us. We'll get through it."

He nodded and stood. "Drink your tea. I'll be right back with food."

Joni drank her tea and munched on her crackers. As her stomach calmed down, her mind settled as well. Perhaps it would be easier for them to work out their new relationship if she stopped fighting against it. Maybe she should give Lex a chance to be what she needed. After all, they'd shared everything in the past, never keeping secrets from each other. Keeping secrets from him was only making things harder than they had to be. She could protect her heart and be open about the pregnancy at the same time.

After taking a sip, she closed her eyes and let the warmth from the tea flow through her body. Although her stomach was still a bit queasy, she was confident she wouldn't need to go racing back to her bathroom. She counted it as a win.

Lex returned with her breakfast. He'd boiled eggs

and made oatmeal, sprinkling brown sugar and sliced strawberries across the top. He'd also brewed her another cup of tea. She smiled. "This looks delicious."

"I didn't want to make anything greasy or with a strong aroma."

"Aren't you going to eat?"

"I hate oatmeal. No matter how much you doctor it with fruit or nuts, it's still oatmeal."

Joni scooped up a large spoonful. "I love it. Especially with fruit in it."

"I remember. You acted like you'd died and gone to heaven when we were in Raleigh for the North Carolina mayors' meeting. You almost knocked over the former mayor of Willow Creek in your haste to get to it."

Joni laughed. "In all fairness, he was blocking my path. Plus he was taking way too long."

"I thought he was moving pretty well for a man of his age."

Joni swallowed another spoonful, then moaned in delight. "This is so good. I feel so spoiled. I could totally get used to this."

"Good, because I'll be making you breakfast in bed every day until this morning sickness passes." He held up his hand, anticipating her protest. "No arguments. I don't mind doing it, and it is most definitely necessary. Certainly you don't prefer being sick every morning, do you?"

"You've got me there. This is a much better way to start the day."

They discussed the details and decided on the best time for him to arrive. He already had a key to her apartment, just as she had a key to his house, so that was one detail they didn't need to work out. Joni swallowed the rest of her tea.

"Do you have time to take me to get my car now?"

"Now? You were just on the verge of passing out half an hour ago."

"I feel better now. Hopefully I'll be okay for the rest of the day."

"You've been sick in the afternoon and evenings before. I've seen you, remember?"

"That's because I wasn't eating right. I'd get busy and then forget to eat. Now that I know what will happen, I'll make sure to eat properly. The doctor recommended that I eat small meals several times a day so that's what I'm going to do."

"If you want, we can stop at the store before we get your car. That way we can get whatever you need. We can put the meals together today so you'll only have to grab and go."

"I don't want to take up your whole day."

"Shopping won't take long."

"In that case, let me get dressed."

He took the tray of dirty dishes. "I'll clean up the kitchen in the meantime."

Joni waited until Lex had closed the door behind him before getting out of the bed. This is what she'd pictured whenever she'd imagined being pregnant. Not the morning sickness, of course. Throwing up every morning didn't have a place in her fantasy. But having her baby's father take care of her needs, including bringing her breakfast in bed, was part of the dream. The only thing missing from the picture was the most important part. Love. She gave herself a mental shake. She couldn't get caught up in fantasies. She needed to stay grounded in reality. Truthfully, the reality might not be what she'd hoped and dreamed of, but it wasn't all bad, either.

Lex loaded the last bag of groceries into the trunk of his car. He couldn't remember the last time he'd had this much fun at the store. Probably never. Even though he and Joni had spent a lot of time together over the years, they'd never gone shopping together. If he'd known what he was missing, he would have insisted on it.

Joni's grandfather had owned a soul-food restaurant on the South Side of Chicago where she'd grown up, and her brother owned a popular restaurant, so when she'd begun to show Lex new ways to make sure the produce was fresh, he'd believed her. After all, with her pedigree she should know. Despite the odd looks he'd gotten from a couple of shoppers, he'd done as she'd instructed. It wasn't until he'd caught her smothering a laugh that he'd realized she'd been pulling his leg.

Without thinking, he'd grabbed her and begun to tickle her. She'd laughed so hard that she'd sent dozens of oranges onto the floor, which for some reason only made her laugh more. Before he knew it, he was laughing too, making it much more difficult to gather and pile the fruit. Fortunately there weren't a lot of people around to see him make a spectacle of himself. Not that witnesses would have ruined the fun. A man couldn't take himself too seriously, even if he was the mayor.

They'd talked and joked as they went from aisle to aisle, and for a while it had been like old times. The only time they'd disagreed was when it came time to pay. Lex had whipped out his debit card and run it through the machine while Joni had been rummaging in her purse trying to find hers. She'd started to argue, but when he'd gestured toward the bagger, she stopped. He knew the last thing she wanted to do was attract attention.

The look Joni had shot him as she'd replaced her debit card let him know the matter wasn't closed. Not that he was worried. He'd been right to pay for the food. Joni was pregnant with his child, and it was his duty to make sure that she had whatever she needed.

He glanced at her. She was sitting in the car, but even though he couldn't see more than her shape, he could still picture her as she'd been laughing. She'd been so vibrant. With her skin glowing and her eyes sparkling, she'd been the sexiest woman he'd ever seen. Just recalling how she'd looked had his blood heating.

He slammed the trunk shut, wishing it was as easy to shut the door on his lust. No matter how hard he tried to control his thoughts, desire would burst through at the most inconvenient time. But then, anytime he was lusting after Joni was the wrong time. They were only friends, and he needed that relationship to work. Somehow or other he had to get a hold of his feelings. He looked up at the sky for guidance that wasn't there and then got in the car.

Joni was eating a candy bar. She gave him a dirty look but otherwise didn't react. Good. He really didn't want to ruin what had otherwise been a good morning by arguing over money. "You want me to drop you at your car now?"

"Yes."

The drive was short; they were at the youth center in about ten minutes. When they got there, she jumped out of the car before he could open her door. She dug out her keys and stalked to her car, then unlocked the door and got inside. But he held the door before she could close it. "Are we okay, Joni?"

"I told you before, I have money."

"I know that."

"When you insist on paying for things I should provide for myself, I feel like you are treating me like a child. And when you ignore my feelings, it makes me angry."

"That's not my intention. To be honest I never looked at it that way."

"No? Then, how are you looking at it?"

"The way I see it, you're doing so much more than I ever could. Twenty-four hours a day, seven days a week, you're taking care of the baby. I'm not doing anything. I'm barely around. To me, the least I can do is pay for your food. It never occurred to me that I was offending you."

She sighed. "I know. But regardless of your intentions, that's how I feel."

One step forward, two steps back. "I'm sorry. I'll try to do better."

"Okay."

He followed her home, trying to keep his focus. He'd made so many mistakes without meaning to. Being around Joni these days was like walking through a minefield. One wrong step and the relationship was blown to pieces. Caroline had been emotional and frequently illogical when she'd been pregnant, too. He'd forgotten about that. But they'd been married, so money had never been an issue. She hadn't gotten upset when he'd paid for necessities. But other things had made her erupt for no reason. Perhaps it was going to be the same way with Joni. As long as the baby was healthy, Lex would deal with it. And the baby had to be okay. He couldn't bear to think about what his life would be like if something happened to his child.

When they got back to Joni's place, he parked and opened his trunk. As he'd expected, she grabbed a couple of bags and started up the stairs. Lex knew better than to make a fuss, so he picked up the rest and followed her. By the time he reached the door, she'd already opened it, so they went inside and unloaded the groceries.

Once the food was put away, Joni heated a can of soup and made them each a sandwich. They carried their plates to the living room and sat on the couch together. Joni slipped off her shoes and tucked her legs under her. "See, I'm perfectly capable of taking care of myself."

He nodded. There was no way he was going to argue with her. She seemed satisfied with his nonresponse and spooned soup into her mouth. Watching her eat shouldn't have aroused him, but it did. Suddenly he was recalling how good it felt to kiss her. Her lips had been so soft and responsive. She'd tasted of wedding cake, champagne and her own sweetness. Though they'd only had that one night, his life had been forever changed. He would never forget the way they'd been together. The feel of her in his arms had been indelibly marked on his soul. But seeing how much damage he'd done to their relationship and how hard it was to get back on good terms, the memory would have to be enough. He couldn't risk losing her, possibly permanently, especially now that they were going to have a child together.

After lunch, Joni announced that she had work she needed to get done. Lex could take a hint, so despite the fact that he was enjoying Joni's company, he stood. When she insisted that she could make her own dinner, he didn't argue, although he didn't like it.

"Thanks for everything," she said as they walked to the front door.

"I'll be back in the morning to make your breakfast. Call me if you need anything before then." He told himself to leave, but instead of turning and going through the door, Lex bent down and kissed her.

He'd only intended to kiss her briefly, but the second his lips met hers, the desire he'd tried so hard to keep in check broke free. He wrapped her in his arms and kissed her deeply. She responded and for a brief moment all was right in his world.

Then she pulled back and he immediately released her.

"Don't do that. I know we kissed each other a couple of times before, but we shouldn't do it again."

There was nothing to say to that. He'd already known better than to touch her in that way. And yet he yearned to kiss her again. And again. He wouldn't, though. He had too much to lose. He was still trying to regain the friendship they'd lost. Any attempt at a romantic relationship would be a big mistake.

Even so, he couldn't continue to go on this way, on the outside looking in. He needed to take care of Joni and his child, but he couldn't do that from a distance.

He needed to be with them all the time. Now all he had to do was find a way to convince Joni of that— sooner rather than later.

Chapter Eleven

Monday evening, Joni dropped her purse on the sofa and then took a shower and changed out of her shorts and into a sundress. She wanted to make dinner for herself to prove that she could do it, but she'd overdone it at work. After pulling out the makings for a salad she ran out of energy and needed a break. She'd just sat at the breakfast bar when there was a knock on her door.

Heaving to her feet, she crossed the room and opened the door. Lex was standing there. "Why didn't you just come in? You have a key."

"It's one thing to just walk in to make breakfast for you when you're supposed to be in bed. It's another to let myself in when I know you're able to come to the door. I'm trying to respect your boundaries."

Obviously he didn't know how exhausted she was

at the end of the day. "Thanks, but feel free to come on in."

Although Joni had every intention of telling Lex she no longer needed him to make dinner, that wasn't the case tonight, so she sat at the counter and watched while he cooked. Besides, he'd come all this way to help her. No matter how badly she wanted to deny it, she was glad he was here. She was beginning to enjoy being with him again. And that was a problem. The more time they spent together, the greater the danger of her falling for him again.

After sitting for a few minutes, Joni decided she had enough energy to make the salad, so she went back into the kitchen to help. Perhaps keeping busy would work as a distraction. After a minute she knew she'd made a tactical error. The room was small, and they had to work around each other. Each time she bumped into Lex, the contact sent shivers skipping down her spine. Once, he put his hand on her waist, and her skin burned from the contact. This was ridiculous. Over the years, they'd touched each other many times without her feeling this kind of awareness. It didn't make sense that one night together had changed the way her body reacted to his.

She needed to get a grip and fast. They were going to be around each other for the rest of their lives. There would be birthday parties and school programs. Swim meets and graduations. Not to mention the day-to-day activities where they'd be in close proximity. She couldn't get all hot and bothered every time they touched, so she needed to put an end to it now—before she went out of her mind.

When he was done cooking dinner, they filled

their plates and sat at the counter to eat. They didn't talk about anything personal, which helped Joni immensely. Actually, Lex seemed distracted, and she wondered if it was work. No. He would have mentioned that. Maybe it was personal. Maybe that Alana Kane had managed to get her claws into him, and he was trying to figure out a way to let Joni know. Her heart plunged to her feet, and she tried to brush the idea aside. Alana wasn't Lex's type. He didn't even seem to like her. Still, something was bothering him.

The thoughts roiled Joni's stomach, and she couldn't eat another bite. Lex didn't have much of an appetite either, so he wrapped up Joni's leftovers, tossed his remains in the trash and loaded the dishwasher. She thought he might leave, but he sat on the sofa and patted the seat beside him.

"Let's talk," Lex said when they were seated.

Joni dropped the remote she had just picked up without turning on the television. She twisted around so she could look him in the eye. From the expression on his face, whatever he wanted to talk about was serious. Her heart thudded in her chest, but she tried to remain outwardly calm. "Sure. About what?"

"I've been thinking about us."

His voice didn't give anything away, so she gave a noncommittal reply. "Okay."

He didn't say anything else but rather drummed his fingers against his thighs, a clear sign that he was nervous. Joni could count on one hand the times she'd seen Lex this uncomfortable in all the years she'd known him. Finally, stomach churning and nerves stretched to the breaking point, she snapped, "Just spit it out already."

Lex gave her an odd look, letting her know that she'd been abrupt. Then he cleared his throat. "We've been spending a lot of time together lately," he finally said. "And we've been getting along well. You need help in the mornings, and I'm more than able to provide it. We're going to be parents soon. I think we should get married."

"What?"

"I think we should get married."

Joni pressed her hands against her temples and then shook her head. She wasn't sure whether she was trying to clear Lex's words from her mind or whether she was telling him no. Of all the things she'd expected Lex to say, this half-hearted marriage proposal wasn't it.

He was so dispassionate, he might as well be asking her what color he should paint his powder room. No, they'd had that conversation when he'd finally begun to decorate his house last year. They'd had a spirited discussion over whether it should be her choice of dark brown or his choice of boring beige. She'd won. And why was she even thinking about that now? While momentarily distracting, the memory couldn't take away the sting of his loveless, emotionless joke of a proposal.

"Don't say no right away. Just listen."

"Why? I'll still say no to this crazy idea."

"It's not crazy when you think about it. We get along well. I know things have been awkward between us lately, and I take total blame for that. But we're getting past that. The biggest part of marriage is friendship. And you, Joni, are probably the best friend that I've ever had. We have a similar outlook on life. Neither of us takes ourselves too seriously."

"True. And that's why we were great friends. But that doesn't mean we'd be happy married to each other." The one time they'd tried to be more than friends had ended in a disaster too painful for her to discuss with anyone—especially him. She couldn't believe he'd forgotten about that already.

"I think we would. And think about our child. He or she would be so much happier living with both parents instead of going back and forth between our homes."

"That's not reason enough to get married. As long as we don't bad-mouth each other, our child will be happy. As you said, we're friends. That's all that's necessary."

To Lex, it was all so simple. But he was missing the most important thing. Love. Joni couldn't imagine being in a loveless marriage, even for the sake of her child. She wanted more from a spouse and believed that eventually he would, too. They might start out as friends but end up as enemies. And even if they didn't, there was no way she wouldn't end up heartbroken.

"Joni."

"I can't, Lex. I don't think it'll work. Being friends is great, but it takes more than that to make a marriage work. But we can still raise this baby together."

"But how will I keep you guys safe?"

"From what?"

"From everything. What if you get sick one night and can't take care of the baby? Or what if the baby gets sick?" The fear in Lex's voice struck Joni's heart. He sounded slightly irrational, something she'd never expected from him. This pregnancy was revealing all kinds of things she'd never known about him.

"I'm fine, Lex. The baby's fine, too. My pregnancy is progressing normally."

"That could change any minute."

"Lex." Joni reached out to soothe him. She'd never seen him so worried.

He took her hand, a pained look on his face. "I had a child before. A sweet baby girl who died when she was only four weeks old."

Joni's heart stopped. Lex had had a child? When? She'd known he was divorced, but he'd never once mentioned losing a child. So many questions swirled through her mind. She thought that they'd shared everything. She'd certainly told Lex every secret of hers, including her most painful ones. She'd cried on his shoulder as she'd told him how hurt she'd been when her former fiancé confessed to being a cheating jerk. That pain was nothing compared to how betrayed she felt realizing that Lex had kept a secret from her.

Apparently they hadn't been as close as Joni had believed. Perhaps their entire friendship had been a figment of her imagination. She'd thought they were confiding everything in each other, but she'd been the only one. He'd kept secrets.

"When? How did your baby die?"

"I was away on a business trip. My ex-wife called me and told me that Briana had died in her sleep. There was no explanation."

"Crib death?"

"There was no explanation. All I know is that my baby is gone." His voice was flat as if the pain was so severe that showing the slightest emotion put him at risk of breaking down.

"I'm so sorry for your loss. That must have been devastating."

"There's no pain like losing a child. If only I'd been there, I might have been able to prevent it."

"I don't know much about sudden infant death syndrome, if that's what this was, but I don't think it works that way. You could have been there and sadly your baby still could have died. It's not your fault, Lex."

"I was her father. I was supposed to take care of her."

"And knowing you, I'm sure you did. But there are some things that a parent can't protect against. This is one of them."

"If I had been there, I might have gone into her room and noticed that she wasn't breathing."

There would be no convincing him otherwise, so she didn't bother to argue with him. "When did this happen?"

"Seven years ago."

That was about a year before he'd moved to Sweet Briar. Had he been running away from the pain? Not that she blamed him. She'd moved from Chicago shortly after her engagement imploded. But that hadn't been a secret. Lex knew it all. He'd seen her agony. Yet he'd kept his pain hidden from her. Even so, she felt bad for him. "I'm sorry."

"But if we're married and live together, I'll always be there."

"I'm sorry, Lex, but that's not a good enough reason to get married. I promise you I'll take care of our baby when you aren't around. And I know you'll do the same when I'm not around. That's the best I can do because I won't marry you. I've heard your arguments, and my answer is no. And it's going to stay no."

His shoulders fell, but then as he rallied they straightened. Standing, he walked to the door and then looked back at her. "Think about it. Getting married is the perfect answer. The only answer. That's the only way I'll be able to take care of both of you."

"No, it's not. Your fear is controlling you, and you're unable to see the truth."

"You need more time to think about this, so I'll leave. I'll see you in the morning."

Joni nodded, keeping a forced smile on her face until the door closed behind Lex and she heard him descend the stairs. Once she was sure he was gone, Joni burst into tears. She couldn't believe Lex would actually propose a marriage of convenience. He knew how much having a loving marriage meant to her. She'd told him more than once how she longed to have the kind a marriage her parents had. She'd shared with him how hurt and disappointed she'd been to discover the man she'd planned to marry had been a liar. Yet he'd ignored all that and suggested that she settle for less than she wanted in order to keep himself happy. He'd put his needs ahead of hers. But then, he wasn't in love with her, so why would he sacrifice for her?

She understood that his pain over losing his child must have been excruciating and that right now he was terrified of losing their baby. Just thinking of it scared her near to death. But she couldn't let that fear rule her. And she certainly wasn't going to let it drive her into Lex's arms when love wasn't part of the bargain. Oh, how she wished love had been part of the deal!

Leaning on Lex had been a mistake. She'd let down

her guard, and he'd slipped back into her heart, leaving her in a place where it would be so easy to fall in love with him. That was a mistake she intended to correct before it was too late. She was going back to her original plan. She was going to stay away from him as much as she could until the baby was born.

Lex stared into his glass. He'd long since finished drinking the soda, but he didn't have the strength to put the glass on the table. She'd said no. Just *no*. Lex had expected Joni to be resistant at first—his proposal had come out of the blue, after all—but he'd thought she'd come around. To him it made perfect sense to get married. Until a couple of months ago, they'd been the perfect couple. Except they hadn't actually been a couple. Theirs hadn't been a romance. They'd been friends. They still would be if he'd had the ability to control his desire.

Sighing, he set the glass on the coffee table. There was no going back and no way of changing things. The only way was forward. They'd created a child. A child that he was going to have to protect. But how could he do that if he wasn't around?

Lex closed his eyes. Even after all this time, he could hear Caroline's screams. Over and over she'd said that he hadn't been there when the baby had died. Though the doctor had said his presence wouldn't have changed anything, Lex didn't believe it. And the fact remained—he hadn't been there. Later Caroline had apologized, saying she'd been distraught and didn't blame him, but he'd known she was only mouthing words. He knew she'd held him accountable in her heart. Whether or not she'd meant what she'd said, the damage had been done. Their marriage had suffered. A year after Briana's death, Caroline and Lex were divorced. Eventually he'd stopped loving her and let go of the pain he'd felt when his marriage ended.

But he'd never been able to let go of the pain from losing his baby girl. His heart didn't ache every day like it used to, and his memories of her were filled with fondness, but the sadness was still a part of his soul. He'd thought he'd overcome the fear, but it was attacking him ferociously. Whenever he thought of his and Joni's baby, his joy was tempered by fear. And the fear was growing and becoming more unmanageable.

Rationally he knew it was wrong to be upset with Joni for rejecting his proposal, but that didn't change the fact that he was. Not only because he wanted to be with his child; part of him wanted to be with Joni, too. Her absence from his life was painful. Even when they were together, which wasn't as much as he'd like, he was aware that they weren't as close as they used to be. Getting married would solve that problem by giving them the chance to grow close again. Now they never would.

One thing was clear. He couldn't be a good father to his child if he was still afraid. If he didn't get a handle on his fear, he was going to blow it. He might not mean to, but the thought that he might withhold his love in order to protect his heart sent chills through him. That would be wrong in every imaginable way.

Lex knew what he had to do. He had to go back to New York and face the painful past he'd tried to leave behind. Of course, he couldn't go now when Joni needed him. He wanted to make sure her days started out well. And that gave him the opportunity to spend time with her. If she got used to having him around, it would be easier to convince her to marry him. And getting married was the right thing to do. With enough time, Joni would come to realize that. He just needed to wait her out.

Chapter Twelve

Joni opened her eyes and sat up. Smiling, she got out of her bed and did a little jig. Yesterday she'd awakened without feeling the least bit sick. She'd been worried it might be a fluke, but it hadn't been. Dr. Starkey had been right. The morning sickness had passed. Having breakfast in bed had been a big help. For the past ten days, Lex had brought her light meals that she'd eaten before putting a foot on the floor. Then, although he'd tried to linger, she'd managed to shoo him away as soon as they'd eaten. She would have preferred he not stay to eat with her, but considering he was helping her, that would have been ungracious.

A couple of times she'd caught herself being charmed by him, but she'd put on the brakes before she'd gotten carried away. Limiting her contact with Lex wouldn't protect her heart if she fell under his spell when they were together, which sadly was easy to do. Being around him reminded her of all the reasons she'd always liked him.

Just to be on the safe side, before showering and going into the kitchen, she ate the apple she'd put on her bedside table last night. Feeling adventurous, she decided to make an omelet. She was grating cheddar cheese when she heard the front door open. Turning, she looked around as Lex stepped into the room. Despite all the lectures she'd given herself, her pulse kicked up. Dressed in navy slacks, a pin-striped shirt and a tie, he looked delectable. He might look good, but he was bad for her heart. "Hey."

He grinned. "You're up again."

"Two days in a row. I can safely say that my morning sickness has passed."

"That's good to know."

"I bet you're probably tired of coming over here to cook for me all the time."

"You'd lose that bet. I like starting my day with you. If I had it my way, we'd start and finish every day together."

"Don't start, Lex." For the past ten days Lex hadn't mentioned marriage directly, but he'd dropped a couple of not-too-subtle hints. She'd ignored them. Apparently that hadn't been the right approach, if he still thought he could persuade her to enter into a loveless marriage.

"I'm just saying it makes perfect sense for us to raise our child together."

She frowned and put down the grater. "I was going to invite you to stay for breakfast, but I'm about to change my mind. We're friends, Lex. Period and end of discussion." Considering how much she'd hated him before, being friends was a big step.

"I don't want to argue."

"Neither do I. But I don't want to have this conversation again, either."

He nodded, then picked up a knife and began slicing tomatoes. "Okay."

They didn't talk as they worked, and although the silence wasn't as comfortable as she would have liked, it wasn't uncomfortable either. Maybe he'd gotten the message this time.

When they'd finished eating, Lex turned to her. "Since you're better and don't need me to take care of you right now, I'm going to New York for a couple of days."

She hadn't expected that. "Okay. When are you leaving?"

"Probably Saturday, if I can get a flight. I'll only be there for a couple of days. There's something I need to take care of."

Once she would have asked him what it was, but now she wouldn't. If she wanted to keep an emotional distance from him, she had to allow him to do the same. Then again, once he would have just told her. Lex might want to believe they were still solid friends, but she knew there were cracks in the foundation.

"Okay. Have a nice trip." Although she would miss Lex, the separation would do them both good. She needed to get her head and heart on the same page once and for all. Her head knew that marriage would lead to heartbreak, but her foolish heart still held out hope that it could work.

They cleared the dishes and then went their separate ways, a symbol of the future of their relationship.

Lex looked out the airplane window, watching as the buildings began to come into focus. Flying gave him the ability to kill two birds with one stone. He got where he needed to be and could use the time to knock items off his to-do list. While he'd been in the air, he'd gotten some work done, although he hadn't accomplished nearly as much as normal. But then, he wasn't as focused as he usually was. Every once in a while, he'd caught himself thinking about Joni.

The past week and a half had been perfect. There was something intimate about making breakfast for Joni and then bringing it to her in bed. Without fail, she'd stretch her arms over her head, and her breasts would rise and pull against her pajama top. No matter how often he'd told himself not to stare, his eyes would automatically gravitate to the sight. Lucky for him, she'd never once caught him. He could only imagine how disastrous that would have been. It had taken too long to get back into her good graces to make the mistake of letting their relationship become sexual again. She'd only recently begun to consider him a friend. He had to clamp down on his desire, no matter what it took.

The plane landed and sped down the runway. After the pilot slowed the plane, he taxied to the gate. Once the door opened, people flooded the center aisle. Years of travel had taught Lex that jostling for position in the aisle was more frustrating than allowing others to exit before him. The minute or so that passed between the first and last passenger getting off wasn't worth the tension that stayed with him long after he'd left the airport.

Once most people had deplaned, Lex grabbed his bags, thanked the flight crew and walked through La-Guardia. He'd told his parents he was coming to New York, and he was having dinner with them tonight. Initially they'd wanted to invite his brothers, but Lex had asked them not to. He was going to the cemetery first and wouldn't be in the mood to be around a lot of people afterward, even his brothers.

Lex had reserved a car, so he went to the exit where his driver was waiting. After his suitcase was loaded into the trunk, Lex gave the chauffeur the address, then sat back in his seat.

He looked at the empty space beside him and wished that he'd asked Joni to come with him. Facing his past would have been so much easier if she was with him. He'd been tempted but hadn't let the words he'd held in his heart come out of his mouth. Even though she'd gone for a few days without experiencing morning sickness, he didn't want her flying unless it was absolutely necessary.

Lex had brought work with him, but his briefcase remained closed. With his emotions churning inside him, he wouldn't be able to concentrate, so he stared out the window and watched as the city sped by. He loved New York. There was an energy that fed his soul. It wasn't just the people, although they were a part of it. There was a buzz in the air that was an actual part of the city. He'd never felt it anywhere else. After Briana's death, the atmosphere had felt wrong. How could the city continue to vibrate with life when his little girl no longer breathed? How dare the birds continue to fly when his sweet baby could no longer see them? Everything about New York had begun to feel wrong. All of the life was suffocating him.

His marriage had begun to die, too. Once he and Caroline had loved each other passionately. Briana's death had hurt them each deeply, but rather than turn to each other, they'd mourned alone and drifted apart, eventually getting a divorce.

Then New York had begun to feel oppressive. He'd started putting in even longer hours at work, traveling nonstop around the globe, but he couldn't escape the overwhelming grief that followed him. Finally he'd quit his job and moved to North Carolina. After watching the town slowly go under, he'd run for mayor and helped to turn things around. As he had worked, most of the pieces of his life had grown back. When Joni moved to town, they'd become close friends, and he'd learned to laugh again. But he realized now that he'd simply buried the sorrow and fear that had accompanied his baby's death. Rather than deal with the heartbreak, he'd papered over it. Now it was breaking free. He had to face the agony now so that he could be a good father to his unborn child. And hopefully once he'd faced his past, he'd be able to fall in love again.

The car reached the cemetery and went through the gates. Though he hadn't been back since the day they'd put his little girl in the ground, he knew exactly where her grave was located. As he directed the driver down the winding road, Lex's heart was pounding, and he began to sweat. He didn't want to do this. But in order to go forward, he had to face the past.

When they reached the area where Briana was buried, he had the driver pull over. Lex had brought a tiny teddy bear with him, and he grabbed it from the bag near his feet.

"I won't be long," he told the chauffeur.

The other man looked at the toy in Lex's hand, and his eyes filled with compassion. "Take as long as you need."

Lex couldn't speak past the lump that had suddenly materialized in his throat, so he only nodded. His legs felt heavy as he trudged through the neatly mown grass. Mature trees were spaced throughout the grounds, and if not for the headstones, the cemetery could have been mistaken for a park. A serene setting had been very important to him. He couldn't imagine leaving his child someplace that didn't look happy, and he'd rejected two gloomy, depressing cemeteries, even though they'd been closer to home.

As he wove his way around the graves, his eyes began to burn, and his vision began to blur. He blinked, but his vision didn't clear. All he'd done was force the moisture from his eyes, sending tears down his face. He wiped them away, but they continued to come. Faster. The closer he got to his daughter's final resting place, the harder they fell. By the time he reached her headstone, his face was completely wet, and he'd given up on trying not to cry.

His little girl was dead. He'd never hold her again. If that didn't warrant his tears, he didn't know what did. He let the tears and the sorrow come. This was the first time in seven years that he'd allowed himself to fully grieve. His chest heaved as he recalled the agonizing moment at the funeral when they'd closed the coffin on his sweet little angel for the last time. He'd insisted on being a pallbearer, and as he'd carried her tiny coffin from the church to the hearse, he'd remained stoic. He'd needed to be strong for Caroline, who'd been inconsolable. She'd sobbed throughout the funeral and in the car on the way to the cemetery. She'd screamed as they'd lowered the casket into the grave, and he'd held her in his arms as she'd cried.

But there was no one here to be strong for now. No need to hold back. Falling to his knees, he let the tears come, hoping they would cleanse him of the pain and guilt. "I'm so sorry, baby. I loved you so much. I should have been able to keep you safe. There should have been a way."

But there hadn't been. The doctors had been unequivocal. Nothing could have prevented her death. His pastor had said that it had been her time to go. Lex hadn't understood it then or now. He probably never would. But he had to accept Briana's death if he was ever going to be whole again. Acceptance was the only way he could move on.

Gradually his vision cleared, and he wiped away the wetness from his face. Reaching out, he touched the words carved in the headstone. *Beloved daughter.* He leaned the teddy bear against the marble and then stood. Though he was sad, he no longer felt the oppressive grief. The emptiness. Perhaps he should have come here sooner. But then he hadn't realized he'd needed to until Joni had told him she was pregnant.

He pictured his little girl as he'd last seen her. He'd been holding her against his chest, singing a song to her. She'd looked up at him and smiled. A real smile. Not gas. She'd been happy. Although Briana hadn't had a long life, she'd been loved every second of it. She'd truly been their beloved daughter. Lex would never understand why she'd been given so little time, but he could content himself with the knowledge that he'd loved her with his entire being.

And he would love his new baby the same way.

After whispering a last goodbye, Lex stood and slowly walked back to the hired car. The driver spotted him and started to get out of the car to open the door, but Lex waved him back to his seat. Once he was inside, Lex gave the driver the address to his parents' house. As he neared Scarsdale, an affluent suburb of New York City, he tapped his foot in anticipation. It had been far too long since he'd seen his parents.

The driver pulled into the circle drive in front of his parents' stately brick house. Lex hopped out of the car, tipped the driver, grabbed his luggage and jogged up the stairs. He pressed the doorbell, and as it chimed inside, he looked around. The house was filled with memories of his childhood and youth. He could almost hear the sounds of his and his brothers' laughter. He recalled the snowball fights they'd had in the front yard with the neighborhood kids. His brothers were younger than he was, and for a while the youngest two hadn't been able to throw far, but Lex had never taken up any of his friends' offers to join forces against his siblings. Family loyalty hadn't permitted him to do something like that, even if it meant losing some battles. Besides, he liked his brothers and wanted them on his side. He'd always hoped to have children who'd be just as close to each other.

When Briana had died, he'd thought that dream had died with her. He couldn't imagine having another child. And yet in just over six months, he would be a father again. This time the joy he felt at the idea wasn't tempered by fear or dread. He truly felt only happiness.

The door swung open, and he turned back around to see his father standing there. Tall with brown skin and more salt than pepper in his hair, Alex Devlin radiated strength. Lex and his brothers had always believed that when their dad was around, things would work out.

They embraced, and then Lex followed his father into the house. Despite the dark wood paneling on the lower half of the walls, the entryway was bright, courtesy of the two-story stained-glass window over the front door. Lex set down his suitcase beside the round table holding a huge vase of vibrant flowers that his mother preferred.

"I was surprised when you said you were coming to New York. Not that we're not glad to see you. It's been too long."

Lex nodded. "I know. I'll do better in the future. This trip was a last-minute thing."

"Is anything wrong?"

"Not really. I just needed to come back. And while I was here, I decided to stop by and see you and Mom."

"Do me a favor, son."

"What's that?"

"Tell your mother that she's the primary reason you came to town. Women don't like taking second place to anything."

Lex laughed. "I think I can do that."

"What can you do?" his mother asked as she came into the room.

"Nothing." Lex hugged his mother. Medium height and slightly overweight, Regina described herself as *pleasingly plump*. She had a quick smile and was warm to everyone. His and his brothers' friends had claimed her as a second mother, and they'd always hung out here. She hadn't minded the crowd or the extra noise. As long as everyone had treated others kindly and respectfully, they'd been welcome.

Although they didn't resemble each other in the slightest, Joni reminded him of his mother. She had the same sweet spirit.

His mother playfully elbowed him in the side. "Like I believe that. You're right on time. I was just about to put dinner on the table."

His parents had renovated the house in the past couple of years, and though it no longer looked like it did when he'd lived here, it felt the same. The kitchen had changed the most. The wall separating the kitchen from the dining room had been knocked down, creating one big room. Counters now ran the entire back wall of the room. A huge quartz island with seating for eight in the middle of the kitchen had replaced the old table. Lex pulled out a chair and sat next to his father.

His mother set a pot roast and potatoes on the island. Rolls and green beans followed. "I hope you're hungry."

"Aren't I always?"

They said grace and began filling their plates. Lex sampled everything, then smiled at his mother. "Delicious as usual. I might have to kidnap you and bring you back to Sweet Briar with me."

His father chuckled. "Oh, no, you don't. If you want to eat like this, then you need to learn to cook."

"Nothing ever tastes as good as Mom's." He turned to his mother. "What do you say?"

"You know I can't leave your father. He can't cook

a lick. But as charming as you are, I'm sure you can find a woman of your own. But you'd better do it before your looks fade."

Clearly amused, his father laughed.

"Mom, that's not very progressive of you."

"Bah. I'm just stating a fact. You're not getting any younger."

Lex shook his head. His parents had been encouraging him to remarry for years. They'd started out giving him subtle hints, but lately they'd gotten more direct. Lex was the oldest, but his brothers were also of marrying age. None of them had taken the plunge, and he wondered if his own failed marriage factored in their decisions.

"I know you were devastated when you lost Briana, and that's perfectly understandable," his mother continued, her voice growing gentle, "but you're missing out on so much that life has to offer. You were a great father, a great husband, and you can be again. You just have to open up that heart of yours to love once more."

She'd said something similar many times in the past. On those occasions, Lex had been angry that his mother had dared to suggest such a thing. Didn't she know how devastated he'd been when he'd lost not only his wife but his child? His everything? Now, though, the words didn't upset him. Perhaps because he'd realized that having another child wouldn't mean he'd forgotten Briana. He'd never do that. But maybe time really had healed his wounded heart and he could love another woman and create another family.

He set down his fork then took a sip of water before smiling at his parents. "Actually, I'm going to be a father next year."

"What?" His parents exchanged surprised glances before looking back at him.

"It's true."

"That's great. But who are you having a child with?" His father's tone was one part stern, one part confused, and for a brief moment Lex felt like a sixteen-year-old telling his dad that he'd gotten his girlfriend in trouble.

"And is there a wedding in your future?" his mother added.

"I'm having a baby with Joni," Lex said, answering his father's question first, since it was the easiest and less painful one.

"Oh, I love Joni. I'm glad to see the two of you have finally figured out that you're perfect for each other. So when is the wedding?" His mother practically levitated at the romance of it all. She might have raised six boys and spent countless hours building go-carts and cheering at their sporting events—she'd actually helped his dad coach his basketball team one season—but she was a hopeless romantic. A relationship with Joni would be a dream come true for her.

"Well, it didn't quite happen like that. Joni and I aren't in love. And we aren't getting married."

"Well, just how did it happen?" The stars in his mother's eyes had turned to daggers. Just like that, he was on her bad list. "How did Joni end up pregnant if you aren't in love with her?"

Lex glanced at his father, who had the exact same expression on his face as his mother. He'd always known his parents loved Joni. He just hadn't realized how deep that love went. Their first loyalty had always been to him, but that wasn't the case now. He'd better start explaining and fast. "Okay. This is what happened. One of Joni's sorority sisters got married a couple of months ago in a four-day affair in Chicago. Joni's ex was going to be there with his new wife, and she asked me to go as her pretend boyfriend. So I did."

"And?" His mother stretched that one word over enough syllables to make an entire paragraph.

"And one thing led to another, and she's pregnant."

"I see," his father said, looking at him hard. The feeling of being sixteen returned.

"And as far as getting married goes, I told her that it would be best for the baby to be raised in a two-parent home. We've always been friends and gotten along well, but she said no." He hated to throw Joni under the bus, but his parents wouldn't get angry with her. Besides, she wasn't the one getting the stink eye. And maybe his parents could persuade Joni to accept his proposal.

"Say what, now?" Lex's dad said, then burst out laughing.

Regina shook her head. "I don't know where we went wrong with you."

"What?" Lex asked. "It makes perfect sense. We're together all the time. Whenever I travel for work or have to attend a function, she always goes with me. Getting married and raising our child together wouldn't change anything."

Clearly exasperated, Regina turned to Lex's dad. "Talk sense into your son, Alex."

"You've been married before. And I know you and Caroline loved each other. Are you telling us that your marriage was simply best friends living together?"

His father's words hit him right in the gut. No, his marriage to Caroline hadn't been like that. They'd been deeply in love. He'd been the best husband to her that he'd known how to be. And when it had ended, he'd been destroyed.

"I'm with Joni," his mother said. "Lots of people co-parent their kids. In fact, if you guys aren't in love, getting married would be an enormous mistake. You could end up hating each other, and that would be disastrous for the child. For all three of you."

"Our friendship is solid," Lex argued, though he wasn't as confident with his plan now as he had been.

"Yes. But what will you do if you meet someone and fall in love?" she asked.

"Not going to happen." He knew that for sure.

"Maybe not, but who's to say Joni won't? She's a beautiful woman with a great personality. I'm sure some man will notice that and sweep her off her feet."

"No."

"What do you mean *no*?" his father asked. His parents had mastered the art of the double team.

Lex didn't reply. He couldn't. He could barely breathe past the band that suddenly tightened around his chest. Joni with another man? That was unthinkable. Unimaginable. And yet, as his mother just pointed out, it was all too possible. Then where would he be? The thought of Joni spending all of her time with another man was painful, but the idea of another man touching her nearly brought him to his knees.

He couldn't imagine a world where he and Joni weren't the most important people in each other's lives. Nor could he picture a time when they didn't share everything. She was the one he wanted to experience everything with, good or bad. The person he wanted to discuss things with. But she was more than his sounding board. More than his best friend. She was the best part of his life. Maybe that's why he wanted to convince her to marry him. Perhaps his subconscious was telling him to hold onto her at all costs.

And with his ridiculous proposal, he'd all but guaranteed that he'd lost her forever.

Lex closed his eyes as realization hit him. He loved Joni. That's the real reason he wanted to marry her. Before she'd come along, he'd been living half a life, pouring all of his energy and emotion into Sweet Briar. Yet when he'd been with Joni, he'd guarded his heart. He'd been attracted to her for a while, but whenever he felt desire, he'd fought against it, telling himself that it was inappropriate. Because they were only friends. And he'd fought against letting her become more than his friend. Being buddies had been safe. She wouldn't be able to break his heart if he kept it from her.

Yet she'd managed to get inside anyway. He had no idea when they'd become more than friends. It had been gradual. Maybe he'd begun falling in love with her in Chicago. Perhaps the pretense had turned into reality. Or maybe he'd been falling in love with her for years. Not that it mattered. He was in love with her. And he'd been too blind to see it.

That was probably why pretending to be in love had been so easy. It had felt natural to act like a besotted boyfriend because he had been besotted. Looking back, he and Joni had been dating for years. Making love had been the next step in their relationship—a relationship that should lead to marriage.

But Joni didn't feel the same way. She'd rejected his proposal without thinking about it. But since the proposal had been lacking in so many ways, that could have been the reason she'd said no, not her lack of feelings for him. Maybe she would have said yes if he'd mentioned love.

He'd messed things up big time, but there had to be a way to redeem himself. He and Joni belonged together. And if she wasn't in love with him now, he'd have to find a way to make her fall in love with him.

He looked up. His parents were staring at him, and he realized he hadn't answered his father's question. It took a moment to even remember what it was. "Joni isn't going to marry anyone else. She's going to marry me."

"Didn't you hear anything your father and I said? A marriage of convenience only works in movies or in books. In real life it would be a disaster."

"I'm not planning on a marriage of convenience. I intend to have a real marriage. You were right, Mom. Joni and I belong together."

"I thought she turned down your marriage proposal," his father said.

"Yes, she did." That was a problem, but not an insurmountable one.

"So what makes you think she'll say yes next time?"

"Because I'm going to ask her the right way. First, though, I'm going to have to win her heart. That shouldn't be too hard because I think she already loves me. At least, I hope so."

"All right, son," his father said, beaming while his mother nodded in approval. "Go get your woman."

That's exactly what he planned to do.

Chapter Thirteen

Joni stared at the plate of waffles and scrambled eggs, then at the empty chair beside her. She was hungry, but she knew the food wouldn't fill the hole inside her. Only Lex could do that, and he wasn't here. She'd woken up this morning with a sinking sensation in her stomach. It hadn't been morning sickness. That hadn't returned. No, it was heartsickness. And loneliness that came from knowing she wouldn't see Lex this morning. Despite her best efforts not to, she'd gotten used to seeing him every morning. She hadn't realized how much she looked forward to starting her day with him.

But that time had come and gone. Now that she was back on her feet, there was no reason for him to come around. Since distance was what she'd wanted, she should be happier. Instead, she was moping around like a lovesick schoolgirl.

He'd called her last night from his parents' house, which was totally unexpected. She figured since this was a quick visit, he'd spend all of his time with his family. Instead, they'd talked and laughed about any and everything for nearly an hour. Lex had always been easygoing, but there was a lightness to him that hadn't been there before.

How had she let herself get attached to him again? That had to be the stupidest thing she'd done in her life.

Pouring syrup on her waffles, she cut them into bite-size pieces and started to eat. Her mood might have affected her appetite, but she'd get nauseous if she didn't eat. Besides, brooding about her feelings wouldn't change anything.

After she finished eating, Joni got dressed and went to work. As usual, she greeted the kids and went to her office. Now that the Sweet Briar Olympics were over, it was time to get to work on her part of the homecoming. She spent a great deal of time negotiating with vendors, pressing for the best prices. After spending an hour and a half on the phone, she went to the break room for a glass of orange juice. She was just returning to her office when Nate, the volunteer working at the front desk today, called her name. As she approached him, she noticed a small crowd of women surrounding his desk.

"What's going on?"

At her words, everyone parted and grinned at her.

"These are for you," Nate said. He pointed to an enormous bouquet of flowers.

"What in the world?" She stepped up to the desk and pulled out an envelope from the bouquet. Her hands trembling, she read the card. *Thinking of you. Lex.*

Joni smiled. Despite knowing he hadn't meant anything romantic by this gesture—he was probably trying to convince her to accept his loveless marriage proposal—she couldn't control the hope that flooded her soul. The wall she'd spent so much time building around her heart began to crumble. She didn't know if this was all a game to him or not, but either way, he wasn't playing fair.

"Who are they from?" Donna, one of the volunteers asked, trying to get a peek at the name on the card.

Joni pressed the card against her chest. "A friend."

"Ms. Joni has a secret admirer," one of the teenage girls exclaimed to her friends, and they began chattering. No doubt their young imaginations were conjuring up a gorgeous, mysterious hero for her. Of course, Lex was gorgeous and could outshine any hero that they came up with.

"Yes, and it's going to remain a secret."

"That's so not fair," the teens complained good-naturedly.

Joni picked up the vase, carried it into her office and set it on her desk. The sweet fragrance immediately filled the small room. Sitting in her chair, she leaned back and let the scent carry her away.

"So, who's the mystery man?" Carmen asked from the doorway. "And does Lex know he has competition?"

Joni waved her best friend into the office. "Have a seat."

Carmen stepped inside, closing the door behind her. "Well? Spill, my friend."

"What makes you think Lex would care?" Joni asked, stalling for time. Or was she looking for reassurance? After all, Carmen was friends with both Joni and Lex.

"Oh, come on, Jocelyn Nicole," Carmen said. Maybe being a mother made Carmen think that using both Joni's names would make her give up the information. Surprisingly enough, it worked. Maybe there was something to it.

"Well, Carmen *Taylor*," Joni replied, joining in the middle name game, "if you must know, they are from Lex."

"Really?" Carmen grinned and clapped her hands. "So he finally decided to make his move. It's about time. Everyone else could tell what was going on."

"Who is *everyone*, and what do they think is going on?" The last thing Joni wanted was to be the subject of gossip. Especially now. Eventually everyone would know that she was pregnant. She wouldn't be able to hide her body under loose clothing for much longer. But she would deal with that when the time came.

"*Everyone* is your friends. And we've been speculating about when you and Lex would finally see what we all can see. You're made for each other."

"We're friends."

"That's a good start. Much better than the one Trent and I had."

Trent had hated Carmen when she'd moved back to town a few years ago. He'd blamed her for the death of his first wife in an accident, even though Carmen had only been a passenger in the car that had collided with his late wife's vehicle. But his daughters had loved Carmen, and eventually Trent had fallen in love, too.

"Sometimes. But other times you get caught in the friend zone and can't find your way out."

"Do you want a way out?"

"I don't know. It's safer there." Or rather, it had been. Now she wasn't so sure.

Carmen looked at her watch and stood. "Safety is overrated. Take a leap of faith."

Joni watched her friend leave. If only it was that easy. It was hard to make that jump when you weren't sure the other person would catch you.

Once word of the bouquet spread through the center, every female over twelve came to the office to see it. Her life must be pretty boring if getting flowers was breaking news. Fortunately nobody pressed her for information about the sender, although another group of teenage girls waxed fanciful about who the secret admirer might be. They peppered her with suggestions, ranging from an undercover prince to the movie star who'd passed through town a week ago. Oddly enough, none of them even mentioned Lex. To them he was just the mayor and not swoonworthy. If only they knew.

In all the years that they'd known each other, Lex had never once bought her flowers. Not even for her birthday. Of course, their relationship had been strictly platonic, so she wouldn't expect him to. The funny thing was, he'd given her other gifts that might have seemed personal if she'd gotten them from another man. Lex had given her bottles of exquisite perfume for Christmas or her birthday or just because, but since his family owned a cosmetics company, that wasn't out of the ordinary. But he'd often shown up at her house with gourmet candy and expensive bottles of wine for no reason at all. Had all of those gifts actually meant something more? No. She wasn't going to rewrite history to soothe her battered heart.

Once her workday was over, Joni loaded the vase of flowers into her car to take them home. When she was inside her apartment, she placed them on her bedroom dresser, where they would be the last thing she saw at night and the first thing she saw in the morning. Then she went into the kitchen to start dinner.

While rice boiled, she chopped broccoli and sliced chicken breasts for a quick stir-fry. She was settling onto her sofa with her plate when there was a knock on her door. Telling herself not to jump to conclusions, she peered out her peephole. Her heart began to pound as she opened the door.

"Lex. I wasn't expecting to see you tonight."

He held up a bag with fragrant aromas wafting from it. "I picked up dinner. Hungry?"

"I made a stir-fry, but that smells better."

"It should. I stopped by Heaven on Earth. You can save it for tomorrow if you want."

"Not a chance. I've been missing their food."

Lex grabbed clean dishes, while she placed her chicken and broccoli into a bowl and put it into the refrigerator. Her mouth watered as she grabbed her plate of pistachio-crusted salmon with glazed vegetables. Once they'd sat down, Joni looked at him. "What are you doing back so soon? I thought you might stay a couple more days."

"I missed you." He forked some carrots into his mouth.

"Oh." Her skin tingled at his simply spoken words. "Okay. How are your parents?"

"Fine." He hesitated. "I told them about the baby. They're excited."

"You what?" A seed of panic sprouted inside her.

"Don't worry. I swore them to secrecy. They won't even tell my brothers."

She wasn't worried about that. Joni knew his parents would respect their privacy. But she couldn't help but wonder how they really felt about the situation. That's why she hadn't been ready to share the information. She breathed deeply. There was no sense getting upset. The cat was out of the bag now.

"They're excited to be grandparents," Lex continued as if he could still read her mind. "They'll be visiting Sweet Briar quite often in the next few years."

"Okay." The panic dissipated.

"Have you thought about telling your parents?"

"I'm not ready."

"What are you waiting on?"

Joni shrugged. She'd tried to picture that conversation but couldn't. Not that her parents wouldn't love her child. She knew they'd be just as happy as Lex's parents were. But still, something held her back.

"That's just not something I want to talk about over the phone."

"I understand. Maybe you can tell them next weekend when we go to Pamela and Edwin's anniversary party."

"What do you mean *we*?" Pamela was Joni's sorority sister and a good friend. Pamela and Edwin had eloped to Las Vegas, so they were throwing a big party to celebrate their fifth anniversary.

"I mean you and me. We told them that we would

be there for the weekend. I imagine they've already reserved our hotel room."

"But that was before."

"Before when? It was nine weeks ago."

"Ten," she corrected automatically.

"Okay. Ten. But we still told them we'd be coming back for their party. They'll be expecting us."

"I can go by myself. I'll make your excuses."

"And just what would that excuse be?" Lex raised his eyebrow.

She chewed, then swallowed her food. "I don't know. You're the mayor. Maybe there was some big crisis that you needed to attend to."

"Not likely. And I'm assuming your friends know how to use Al Gore's Internet. What will they think when they can't find any mention of a crisis?"

"They won't look. They'll take me at my word."

"Even Darrin and Trina? Really? I saw the way he was looking at you. If there's a man who can't believe a woman can ever get over him, he's it. Although, the way I see it, he was lucky to have convinced you he was worthy of your love."

Lex's words stirred warmth in her heart. He was right. She'd been too good for Darrin. She just wished she'd known that *before* she'd asked Lex to pretend to be in love with her.

"It doesn't matter. I'm happy with my life and what I've achieved. I don't need to impress him or anyone else. Let him think I'm still pining after him. I don't care."

"So what's your plan? Are you just going to go there and tell everyone it was all a lie? Are you going to tell your sorority sisters and other friends that you made fools of them?"

She could, but that would only cause drama, taking the focus away from the happy couple on their special day. "No. I'll just tell them that we broke up."

"After all the pretending we did? They'll never believe it."

"They will when I tell them that you were a jerk."

"Okay. And I'll tell them I realize I made a mistake and I want to win you back."

"Wait. What?"

"You heard me."

"But you don't need to come. You don't have a role to play any longer."

"That's your opinion."

"That's the *truth*. Besides, you're not invited."

"*Au contraire*," Lex said smugly. "Edwin and I hit it off, and he personally invited me for the weekend."

"That's because he thought we were dating."

Lex grinned devilishly. "Whatever the reason, I'm going."

She had to make him see reason. "Lex, we can't pretend anymore. That's what got us into the mess we're in right now."

"What mess is that?"

She pointed at her no-longer-flat stomach. How could he be so clueless?

His smile fled, and he stared at her. His eyes burned with intensity. "Our child is not a *mess*. We might not have intended to create a baby, but that doesn't mean I don't already love him or her."

Her throat clogged with emotion. "I love our baby,

too. I just don't want things between us to get more confusing."

"You're the only one who's confused, Joni. Everything is perfectly clear to me."

That was because he was looking at everything simplistically. Unemotionally. He wanted to get married because of the baby and continue on as friends. He had no idea how easy it would be to agree to his ridiculous plan. But she knew what heartbreak felt like, and she wasn't going to put out the welcome mat. She might not know everything, but she knew marrying a man who wasn't in love with her would be sending heartache an engraved invitation.

She chose not to address his comment and returned to the matter at hand. "Fine. You can go with me."

"And our room? Will we be sharing or not?"

It would raise suspicion if they didn't. What was that crazy saying? *In for a penny, in for a pound*? "Fine. We'll pretend that we're still a couple. We'll share the room."

Chapter Fourteen

Lex watched Joni as she slept, his heart swelling with emotion. For a while he'd been worried she wouldn't let him accompany her this weekend. He'd done some fast-talking and bluffing. He wouldn't have followed her if she really hadn't wanted him to come. She deserved to have a fun time with her friends. If she hadn't relented, he would have just come up with another tactic.

He'd blown it big time with that lame proposal. In fairness, though, he hadn't realized he was in love with her until he'd come close to losing her. Being friends had been safe. He could be around her without having to risk his heart. Only, friendship wasn't enough now. He loved her and was willing to put it all on the line to win her heart. Hopefully being in Chicago, the place where it had all begun, would rekindle her feelings. He just wondered how much damage he'd done to her heart and how hard she would resist to protect herself from being hurt again.

The plane began descending, and he checked to be sure her seat belt was securely fastened, then ordered himself to relax. He couldn't. So much was riding on the next three days, and he wasn't sure he'd be able to pull it off. He shook himself. He'd never let a defeatist attitude get the best of him in the past. He wasn't going to start now when the prize was so great. And what could be greater than marrying the woman you loved and raising a family together?

Joni began to stir as the plane raced toward the runway. When the wheels touched the ground, she opened her eyes and peered at him. Her gaze was a bit fuzzy as if she wasn't quite awake. Then she smiled, and his insides jumped. How could he not have noticed that he'd been falling in love with her? The way his body reacted to her touch, like a live electrical cord had dropped against his skin, should have been his first clue. But then, he hadn't allowed himself the freedom to react until they'd been pretending to be in love.

Or maybe they hadn't been pretending. Maybe that had been the first time they'd been honest about their feelings. Perhaps they'd been pretending to *not* be in love for all those years. He couldn't count the number of instances he'd clamped down on his desire, convincing himself that it was wrong to have those kinds of feelings for her. Now he knew it had only been fear of losing her that had him keeping his distance. He'd wasted so much time. But berating himself meant wasting even more, something he wasn't inclined to do.

"Sorry for falling asleep."

"No worries. I would have gone to sleep myself, but your snoring kept me awake."

Grinning, she poked him in his bicep. "I don't snore."

"Keep telling yourself that."

The plane taxied to the gate and then stopped. The early flight they'd taken was only half-full, so it didn't take them long to deplane. Soon they were walking through the airport. Lex hadn't wanted Joni dragging her suitcase, even though it had wheels, so he'd insisted they check their luggage.

By the time they reached the baggage claim, the other passengers from their flight were clustered around the carousel. After about a minute, the conveyor belt began to move, and the others surged forward. Lex placed a protective arm around Joni's waist and pulled her close.

It felt so good to have an excuse to hold her. He'd had very few opportunities to touch her over the past week. Whenever he'd stopped by the youth center, she'd been busy with the kids. Once she'd been talking with several teenage girls. They'd appeared to be having a serious conversation, so he'd just waved and gone about his business. The other time she'd been leading a sing-along with the preschool and kindergarten crowd. Mesmerized by her beauty and liveliness, he'd hung out in the back of the room, content to watch her.

She stepped away from him. "That's my suitcase."

"I'll get it."

Joni sighed and rolled her eyes at him the same way she'd done when he'd insisted on carrying her luggage to the car. She might feel as strong as usual, but she was pregnant with their precious child. There was no way he'd allow her to do anything that might be of the slightest risk.

Once he had their bags, they picked up their rental car. Although their hotel was located in the heart of downtown Chicago, a short walk or cab ride to everything, Lex liked the flexibility a car gave them. Joni had still been debating about visiting her parents and telling them about the baby when the decision was taken out of her hands. Her parents had already left to spend the week in Wisconsin with friends, giving Joni a reprieve.

Lex unlocked the passenger door for Joni before stowing their suitcases in the trunk and getting behind the wheel. Traffic was slow as they merged with the rest of the cars heading for the expressway. When they were finally on the road, Joni let out a loud sigh.

"In a hurry?" he asked her.

"Not really. I just don't like sitting in traffic. Besides, I'm hungry."

"Do you want to stop and grab something to eat, or would you rather wait until we get to the hotel?"

"Let's go to the hotel first. I know a great restaurant where we can go for lunch. It's not really close-by, but since you rented the car, we may as well use it."

They checked into the hotel and then went up to their room to drop off their bags. Joni went to the bathroom to comb her hair and freshen her lipstick. Lex took one look at the king-size bed and sent a silent thank you to Pamela, who'd reserved rooms for the guests. A moment later, Joni was back. She crooked her finger at him with a wicked smile, and images of the last time they'd shared a room flashed through his mind. They'd put that bed to good use that night. He knew that Joni regretted making love, so he knew there wouldn't be a repeat this weekend. But he was playing the long game. If he made the right moves at the right time, he'd win Joni's heart for good, and they'd spend the rest of their lives together.

"Which way?" Lex asked when they were once more in the car.

"Take a right and then another right."

Lex followed Joni's directions, and thirty minutes later he was pulling into a parking lot next to a red-brick building on the South Side. They walked to the front of the building. Granddad's Soul Food was written in gold letters on the plate-glass window.

"My grandfather started this restaurant a long time ago. He'd hoped to keep it in the family, but it didn't work out that way. My mother became a teacher, and her brother became a doctor. Neither of them wanted the restaurant. Brandon loved hanging out and helping Granddad, but he didn't want the restaurant either, so my grandfather sold it. The new owners use his recipes, so the food is still really good. I would have brought you here before, but with all of my bridesmaid duties, there wasn't time."

The dining room was bigger than Lex had expected. And it was packed. He inhaled, and the aromas made his stomach growl. After a short wait, they were shown to a black leather booth. A waiter immediately brought menus and glasses of ice water.

Lex perused his menu. Everything looked great. "What are you getting?"

"I'm getting fried perch, spaghetti casserole, collard greens, and German chocolate cake for dessert."

"That sounds good."

"Yes. But if you get the fried shrimp, macaroni and cheese, cabbage, and peach cobbler and share it with me, I'll be your best friend."

"You're already my best friend." And soon she would be more than that. Joni might not believe that marriage between friends could work, but to him the friendship was essential. Best friends shared their feelings without fear because they didn't judge each other. They were kind and supportive. They didn't envy. That described their relationship to the letter. And if that wasn't also the definition of love, he didn't know what was. When you added in the sexual attraction, they were a match made in heaven.

"Lex." Joni leaned forward and batted her eyelashes at him. He knew she was being silly by flirting, but it worked. When the waiter returned, he ordered the shrimp and macaroni and cheese instead of the pot roast and mashed potatoes with gravy he really wanted. After all, he was in love.

They laughed as they shared their lunches, which really were as delicious as Joni promised, then returned to their hotel to get ready for the cocktail party for Edwin and Pamela's closest friends on the hotel's roof garden. While Joni showered, Lex prowled the room, trying not to picture her glorious body being pelted by the warm water.

Using a level of self-control that he'd never needed before, he forced the vivid image from his mind and unpacked his suitcase.

After a few more minutes, the bathroom door

opened. Lex turned around and nearly gasped. Joni was standing there dressed in a peach robe that stopped midthigh. She whipped off a shower cap, and her midnight hair tumbled over her shoulders. She was sexiness personified, and she didn't even know it. "I'm done in the bathroom, if you want to take your shower now."

Fearing that his tongue would fall out if he opened his mouth—not that he could speak anyway—Lex nodded and grabbed his shaving kit and clothes. When he stepped into the bathroom, he closed the door and then leaned against it. Wow. That was close. It had taken all of his willpower not to touch her soft skin. Even the most innocent contact would have ignited him, so he'd been careful as he'd stepped around her.

He took a deep breath and got a lungful of rose-scented air. The scent was so familiar it was a part of her. Yet underneath the floral scent was the one that belonged to Joni alone. The one that turned him on.

Stepping into the shower, he quickly washed up and got out. He wrapped a towel around his waist, and after wiping condensation from the mirror, he stood at the sink and trimmed his mustache and beard. He was just finishing when there was a knock on the door. "Yes?"

The door opened a crack, and Joni's head appeared. "Are you decent?"

"About as much as usual."

She laughed and tiptoed inside. "I forgot my makeup bag. I'll get it so you can finish."

"There's room for both of us." He took a step to the side and motioned for her to join him at the sink. Although he had nearly been done, he picked up his scissors and comb and once more began grooming his facial hair. Joni hesitated, then opened her bag and took out her makeup.

After a minute, he put down his tools and, leaning against the counter, watched her get ready. Joni was so beautiful that she didn't use many cosmetics. Not that it would have mattered to him if she did. Whatever a woman did to feel her best was okay with him. Considering that his family made their living by selling cosmetics and perfumes, it would be hypocritical for him to believe otherwise.

She brushed on mascara and blush, then dabbed on lipstick. When she smiled at him, his heart leaped in his chest. Before he could stop himself, he leaned down and kissed her lips, letting his linger for a moment. Her eyes widened, and she inhaled. Their eyes met and held, and he thought she might kiss him back. She lifted a hand toward his face then let it drop without touching him and moved away. "Thanks. I'm done now."

"Okay." As Joni fled, Lex wondered just how far back he'd set their relationship.

Whew. Joni leaned against the wall and waved her hand in front of her face, hoping the slight breeze would help her cool off. When she'd popped her head inside the bathroom door, she'd expected Lex to at least have his pants on. He'd carried his suit bag in with him, after all. And she'd heard him turn off the shower long before she'd knocked on the door, giving him plenty of time to dress. When she saw his muscular bare chest and six-pack abs, her heart had begun to race. She could have backed out when he'd offered to share the space with her, but her silly mind relished the idea of being close to him.

She'd been completely aware of him the whole time she'd been getting ready. With every breath she took, she inhaled his masculine scent. The heat from his body wrapped around her like a lover's arms, tempting her to step closer. Every nerve ending had been on red alert. It was a miracle that her makeup looked okay. With the way her hand had trembled, she'd half expected to look like Bozo's twin sister.

And then he'd kissed her, knocking over the last bricks of the wall around her heart. There was no use denying it any longer. Being angry hadn't worked. Avoiding him—or at least trying to—hadn't diminished her feelings. She was in love with Lex.

She didn't know when it happened. Or how. Perhaps she'd fallen in love with him slowly over the years. Or maybe it happened when they'd made love. Whenever it happened didn't matter. And it didn't change the truth. She didn't hate her best friend. She was in love with him. Now she had to figure out the best way to deal with that problem.

Unfortunately there was no good way. She'd tried kicking him out of her life, but with a baby on the way, that was no longer a viable option. Not that it had worked all that well. Sweet Briar was too small a town, and their lives were too intertwined for that. And truthfully, she really hadn't wanted to do it. She'd tried hard at being just friends, but that had been too confusing. Things they'd once done as friends now took on a new meaning. Even a casual touch suddenly had her burning with desire. Simple comments now contained sexual undertones.

Deciding that fretting wouldn't help, she double-checked her appearance in the mirror over the dresser, wanting to be sure she looked her best. Removing her robe, she smoothed her hand over her dress, brushing away a small wrinkle. The purple dress was strapless and stopped several inches above her knees. It was loose-fitting and disguised her baby bump. She was wearing matching three-inch heels that would make her five feet ten inches. She'd still be several inches shorter than Lex, but the added height gave her confidence. And with her heart now open and vulnerable, she needed every advantage she could get.

She'd pulled herself together by the time Lex stepped back into the bedroom. That control lasted until she turned around and saw him. Dressed in a gray suit and white shirt, he looked like every dream she'd ever had come to life. She felt herself smile and knew that her resistance had been a figment of her imagination. Thankfully, he had no way of knowing that.

"Ready to put on a show for my friends again?" she asked, reminding herself the relationship wasn't real. She had to remember that.

"Absolutely." He held out his arm, and she took it, curling her fingers around his hard muscles. He pressed her hand against his side, and her knees wobbled. As they walked to the elevator, she questioned the wisdom of wearing heels. He flashed her a grin, and the electricity that shot through her body made it clear that the shoes weren't the cause of her imbalance. It was being near Lex and touching him that turned her knees to rubber. She had to remain strong and try to rebuild her emotional wall. Of course, that was going to be hard to do while acting like she was in love with him.

The elevator ride to the rooftop was smooth and quick. The doors opened to reveal large plants scattered across the area, giving the space a tropical feel. Strings of white lights and flickering candles on the beautifully decorated tables added a romantic touch. Joni spotted two of her friends, but before she and Lex could make their way over to them, Madison looked up and then poked Kelly. The two women ran over. Kelly and Madison had also been bridesmaids at Andrea's wedding, so they'd already met Lex. He greeted them by name and then asked about their husbands, also by name. Impressed, Madison pointed across the patio and suggested he join them.

"Sure thing," Lex said before leaning down and kissing Joni. Her eyes closed automatically, and her heart began to beat wildly as his lips lingered over hers. The kiss wasn't overly passionate and was certainly appropriate for a couple who were deeply in love, but even so, Joni felt exposed. Perhaps because, as she returned the brief kiss, she didn't mask her true feelings for him.

Joni's eyes followed him as he crossed the deck to join the other men. When she turned around, Madison and Kelly were grinning at her.

"What?" she asked.

"You guys are so cute together," Kelly said. "I was just wondering how long it would be before we hear your wedding bells. I'm totally ready to sing the sweetheart song again."

Joni couldn't help but glance over at Lex. She caught his eye, and he winked at her. Flushing, she turned back to her friends. Actually being in love meant she didn't have to work hard to convince anyone of her feelings. "I don't know. Give us a little more time to be sure."

"Famous last words," Madison said. "I give you until the end of the summer. I recognize the look in his eyes. That man is in love."

Joni's smile suddenly felt forced. Lex was such a good actor he could have fooled her as easily as he'd fooled her friends. As it was, she'd fooled herself that night months ago. Recalling how painful that had been, she vowed not to make that mistake again. She had to separate fact and fiction.

"Yep," Kelly added. "He'll be proposing soon."

If only they knew he'd proposed already. Too bad that had been the wrong kind of proposal. One built on responsibility and totally lacking in love. One guaranteed to lead to her heartbreak.

"Look who's coming back now," Madison said. "Apparently he can't stand to be away from you more than a few minutes."

Joni smiled when Lex rejoined them, and they began to mingle with the rest of the guests. He was very convincing in his role of the man in love. More than once, Lex whispered in her ear to ask how she felt and if the baby was okay. To her friends it had to look like he was whispering sweet nothings in her ear. To her it was a reminder of why he was with her. The baby was all that mattered to him.

After the reception there was a moonlight cruise on Lake Michigan. As the boat glided across the water, Joni and Lex found a secluded spot and shared a padded bench. A light mist sprayed them every once in a while, but it wasn't unpleasant. The Chicago skyline provided a perfect backdrop for the evening. Before long, the rest of her friends gathered around them, and soon they were reminiscing about their college days. Darrin suffered from seasickness, so to Joni's relief, he and Trina weren't present.

Joni tried to participate in the storytelling, but Lex kept drawing his finger over her bare shoulder, distracting her. His touch felt so good. So right. Everything about the evening felt good, so she decided to enjoy the moment.

She closed her eyes and leaned her head against his shoulder. The sounds of her friends' voices grew dim, and she snuggled closer to Lex. She must have dozed off, because the next thing she knew Lex was whispering in her ear.

"Wake up, baby. We're back at the dock."

"Okay," she replied but didn't open her eyes. Nor did she move. It felt so good to be close to him that she didn't want the moment to end.

"You might have to carry her," a voice said. She recognized it as Madison's and forced her eyes to open. Joni's resistance had limits, and she didn't think it could hold up to being carried in Lex's arms.

"I'm awake." Joni stood and leaned against Lex's side. When he placed his arm around her waist to help her remain upright, she smiled. They might be pretending, but no rule said she couldn't enjoy herself.

The limousine was waiting to drive them back to the hotel. Some of the others were going to gather in the lounge, but Joni begged off. Since everyone had witnessed her taking a nap on the boat, no one gave her any grief. She and Lex said their good-nights and returned to their room.

As soon as the door was locked behind them, Joni grabbed her pajamas and headed for the bathroom. In no time flat, she'd brushed her teeth and washed off her makeup. Predictably, the moment the water splashed on her face, she was wide awake.

When she stepped back into the room, Lex was lounging on the bed. He'd taken off his jacket, tie and shoes, and his feet were crossed at the ankle. He was holding the television remote and was flipping through the channels trying to find something to watch. Joni tossed her dress over the back of the chair and then sat on the other side of the bed. Anticipation made her shiver. She forced the feeling aside, along with the desire that had her perspiring. That same desire had led her astray the last time they'd shared a room. That same desire had led to her broken heart. She hadn't known the danger of giving in to her feelings before. Now she knew and would resist with everything inside her. It was the only way to protect her heart.

"Do you want to watch anything?" Lex asked.

"No. I'm so worn out I'll probably be asleep as soon as my head hits the pillow." That was closer to wishful thinking than the truth. No doubt she'd be awake most of the night trying not to end up in his arms again.

"Okay. In that case, I think I'll watch the Dodgers game. It looks like they might go into extra innings."

Joni nodded, then slid under the sheet. She put her head on the pillow and then glanced at him. He was looking at the TV. It was easier to talk to his profile. "Thanks for coming with me, Lex. I appreciate it. Seeing Darrin and Trina at the cocktail party would have been harder without you."

"I'm enjoying myself."

Joni closed her eyes and listened to the television. Although she wasn't much of a baseball fan, she found the commentator's voice soothing. She snuggled more comfortably in the bed. She wished she could go to sleep beside Lex every night. Unfortunately that wasn't in the cards. At least, not if she wanted to be in a happy, loving marriage, which she did.

Lex knew the exact moment Joni fell asleep because the tension finally slid from her body. He knew she was uncomfortable lying beside him, so he'd tried to keep his distance and be as still as he could. Now that she was finally sleeping peacefully, he no longer felt the need. Some of her hair had fallen across her face, and when he brushed it away, she sighed. If he had his way, he would lie beside her every night for the rest of his life. Somehow he had to convince Joni that they belonged together.

Once she began to snore, he knew that she was in deep sleep, so he took off his slacks and shirt and pulled on his pajama bottoms. Leaning his pillow against the headboard, he settled in and watched the last of the game. When it ended, he switched off the television.

Joni was so close that her sweet scent wrapped around him, and without the distraction of the game, he felt himself being drawn closer. After a while, he turned off the bedside lamp and closed his eyes. Hopefully while he was sleeping, his subconscious mind would come up with a plan to win Joni's heart. Nothing his conscious mind had come up with so far had worked, and he was running out of ideas. He really believed she loved him, so it was frustrating to see how hard she fought against it. He just didn't understand it. Why was she fighting so hard against a love that would make them both happy?

Lex felt a hand pushing against his chest, and instantly awake, he opened his eyes. If his subconscious had come up with a solution for the Joni problem, he'd forgotten it. "Good morning, Joni."

"I'm sorry."

Her apology shocked him. "For what?"

"I'm on your side of the bed."

Technically, yes, but he was holding her in his arms, and their legs were tangled together, so he wasn't complaining. "Okay. But I still have plenty of room."

She shoved against him, and he let her go. Before he knew what was happening, she'd scooted from the bed and run into the bathroom, closing the door behind her.

He raked a hand over his face. What had just happened? Before she'd run away, Lex had seen tears forming in her eyes. He didn't know what he'd done wrong, but he needed to fix it. He'd ask her to forgive him as soon as she came back out.

That was the second time that he'd awakened holding her in his arms, and the second time that he'd needed to apologize. His heart sank as he realized what he'd just thought. The morning after they'd made love, he'd apologized as if he'd done something wrong. But looking back, Joni hadn't appeared offended. She'd seemed dazed, but there had been a happy aura surrounding her. Until he'd apologized. Then all of her joy had disappeared. Reflecting on it now, he realized that he'd hurt her, especially when he'd said they'd made a mistake and should pretend that it had never happened. He'd made her believe he hadn't wanted her, which couldn't be further from the truth.

If only he'd kept his mouth shut and paid more attention to how Joni was acting, things would be different between them. At the time, he'd been so worried about losing her friendship that he hadn't considered the possibility of gaining an even closer relationship with her. One that would make them each so much happier. Seeing the way she'd fled just now, he realized how badly he'd hurt her before. This time she'd apologized first so she wouldn't have to suffer through his apology.

He wasn't going to let it end this way. Nor was he going to let time pass while she berated herself for doing what had come naturally. He was done trying to woo her slowly. That hadn't worked, and if anything, it had confused her and made her doubt his feelings. It was time to act. He was going to declare his feelings once and for all. Right now. And if she didn't believe him today, he was going to tell her over and over again until she did. One thing was certain. He wasn't going to lose her.

When Joni returned, she didn't come near him. Nor did she look at him. So he made the first move, crossing the room and closing the distance between them. If only it was as easy to lessen the emotional chasm separating them. He whispered a prayer, then lifted her chin until their eyes met. Then he said what was in his heart. "I love you, Joni. I want to marry you."

She pulled away and wrapped her arms across

her middle. "Because of the baby. My answer hasn't changed. It's still no."

He reached for her, but she evaded his hands. He blew out a breath. "No, not because of the baby. Because I love you. Because I want to go to bed with you at night and wake up with you in my arms in the morning. Every night and every morning. Because I want to be able to hold you and kiss you all the time, not just when we're trying to convince your friends that we're in love. I want to do all of those things because I am in love with you."

"Since when?" The skepticism written on her face dripped from her voice. His heart ached. He'd done more damage than he'd known.

"I don't know, Joni. I can't put my finger on the exact moment I fell for you. I wish I could because maybe you would believe me. It just happened. It was so subtle that I didn't recognize it right away. I denied my feelings for so long because I didn't want to risk ruining the relationship we had. You're important to me, and I was afraid to lose you. Instead of acknowledging my feelings, I denied they'd changed. Grown. I tried to get things back where they'd been. The place where I knew you cared for me and hopefully always would.

"But you know what I discovered? Feelings grow and change, and that's okay. I love you. And I know you understand what I'm saying because I believe your feelings for me changed. I think you love me, too."

Joni listened as Lex spoke, and the pain in her heart began to lessen. In its place grew warmth and happiness. If Lex had said anything else, she wouldn't have believed him. But his words mirrored her experience.

She believed he loved her because she'd fallen in love with him the same way. It was impossible for her to pinpoint a day on the calendar and say that was when she'd known he was the one, as so many of her friends could do. He'd just been a part of her life so long, a part of her heart for so long, that marking the day her feelings had become more was impossible.

Tears filled her eyes and began to flow down her cheeks. Lex immediately grabbed her hands. "I didn't mean to upset you, Joni."

She looked into his worried eyes. "You didn't. I'm not crying because I'm sad. It's these darn hormones. Or maybe it's what you said. The point is that I love you, too."

He breathed out, and she saw the relief on his face. "I want to marry you. I understand if you want to wait. I'm good with that. And though it's not my preference, we can even co-parent for a while if that's what you need to get rid of your doubts. We'll do this however you want to do it."

Joni laughed. Her heart, which had been weighted down with sorrow only minutes before, felt light. Joyful. "I don't want to wait. To be honest, I'd prefer to get married before the baby is born. All I need is to be married to a man who loves me as much as I love him."

"You can be assured of that." He kissed her deeply, and she felt the love and sincerity in his touch. He pulled back suddenly, and she reached for him again. He held her off for a moment as he looked at the alarm clock. "It's 7:57 a.m."

"Okay. Why did you tell me that?"

"Because neither of us knows exactly when we fell in love. I want to be sure we know the exact minute I proposed." He got on one knee and took her hand into his. "I love you with all my heart and want to spend the rest of my life with you. Will you marry me, Jocelyn Nicole Danielson?"

She answered immediately. "Yes."

"Good. I promise we'll live happily ever after." He stood and kissed her. They were off to a great start.

Epilogue

Nine months later

Lex stood over the crib, watching his son sleep, as he'd done every night for the past three months. It wasn't fear that drove him, but wonder. And love so big his heart couldn't contain it.

"I thought I'd find you in here," Joni said, coming to stand beside him. Her sweet scent encircled him as he wrapped his arm around her waist and pulled her closer. Marrying Joni had been the best decision he'd ever made. The past months had been the happiest of his life. He loved her more each day and would love her for as long as he lived.

She straightened the blanket covering Joshua, one of the many gifts she'd received at her surprise baby shower a few months ago. Joni had been worried that parents would react negatively to her pregnancy and that they would stop bringing their children to the youth center. Nothing Lex had said could convince her otherwise. The dozens of women and teenage girls filling the decorated gym at the youth center and bearing gifts had done the trick and she'd finally relaxed and enjoyed the final months of her pregnancy.

"He's growing so fast. I just don't want to miss a minute."

"You won't. But it's almost one o'clock. If you don't come back to be bed, you'll risk falling asleep tomorrow."

"Not a chance. I'm used to getting up about now." Joshua had only recently begun sleeping though the night. Before then, it had been Lex who'd changed his son's soiled diaper before bringing him to Joni to nurse. Despite the broken sleep, Lex had managed to perform his duties as mayor without a hitch. But Joni wouldn't go back to bed unless he did, so Lex leaned over and kissed his son's forehead then followed Joni from the nursery.

"Are you nervous?" Joni asked as they returned to their bedroom and got into bed.

Tomorrow Lex would be receiving an award from the U. S. Conference of Small Town Mayors. His entire family and hers had come to Sweet Briar for the presentation and the celebration that would follow. "If I say yes, will you kiss me and hold me until I'm no longer scared?"

Joni laughed and put her head on his shoulder. "I'll do that even if you say no."

Lex kissed her soft mouth, letting his lips linger on hers. "That sounds promising."

Sometimes Lex couldn't believe his good fortune. He'd married his best friend and had a son. Life couldn't get much better than that.

* * * * *

Available August 20, 2019

#2713 THE MAVERICK'S WEDDING WAGER
Montana Mavericks: Six Brides for Six Brothers
by Joanna Sims
To escape his father's matchmaking schemes, wealthy rancher Knox Crawford announces a whirlwind wedding to local Genevieve Lawrence. But his very real bride turns out to be more than he bargained for—especially when fake marriage leads to real love!

#2714 HOME TO BLUE STALLION RANCH
Men of the West • by Stella Bagwell
Isabelle Townsend is finally living out her dream of raising horses on the ranch she just purchased in Arizona. But when she clashes with Holt Hollister, the sparks that result could have them both making room in their lives for a new dream.

#2715 THE MARINE'S FAMILY MISSION
Camden Family Secrets • by Victoria Pade
Marine Declan Madison was there for some of the worst—and best—moments of Emmy Tate's life. So when he shows up soon after she's taken custody of her nieces, Emmy isn't sure how to feel. But their attraction can't be ignored... Can Declan get things right this time around?

#2716 A MAN YOU CAN TRUST
Gallant Lake Stories • by Jo McNally
After escaping her abusive ex, Cassie Smith is thankful for a job and a safe place to stay at the Gallant Lake Resort. Nick West makes her nervous with his restless energy, but when he starts teaching her self-defense, Cassie begins to see a future that involves roots and community. But can Nick let go of his own difficult past to give Cassie the freedom she needs?

#2717 THIS TIME FOR KEEPS
Wickham Falls Weddings • by Rochelle Alers
Attorney Nicole Campos hasn't spoken to local mechanic Fletcher Austen since their high school friendship went down in flames over a decade ago. But when her car breaks down during her return to Wickham Falls and Fletcher unexpectedly helps her out with a custody situation in court, they find themselves suddenly wondering if this time is for keeps...

#2718 WHEN YOU LEAST EXPECT IT
The Culhanes of Cedar River • by Helen Lacey
Tess Fuller dreamed of being a mother—but never that one memorable night with her ex-husband would lead to a baby! Despite their shared heartbreak, take-charge rancher Mitch Culhane hasn't ever stopped loving Tess. Now he has the perfect solution: marriage, take two. But unless he can prove he's changed, Tess isn't so sure their love story can have a happily-ever-after...